THE MAN WHO TOOK A BITE OUT OF HIS WIFE AND OTHER STORIES

ABOUT THE AUTHOR

Bev Jafek has published in numerous literary publications, including *Columbia,* the *Black Warrior Review*, and the *Missouri Review*. A former Wallace E. Stegner Fellow in Fiction at Stanford University, she lives in Pelham, New York.

THE MAN WHO TOOK A BITE OUT OF HIS WIFE AND OTHER STORIES

BEV JAFEK

THE OVERLOOK PRESS
WOODSTOCK • NEW YORK

First published in 1993 by
The Overlook Press
Lewis Hollow Road
Woodstock, New York 12498

Acknowledgment is made to the following, in whose pages these stories first appeared: *Bachy*, "The Unsatisfactory Rape"; *Black Warrior Review*, "The Statistician"; *Columbia: A Magazine of Poetry & Prose*, "Schrödinger's Cat" and "You've Come a Long Way, Mickey Mouse"; *Cutbank*, "There's a Phantom in My Word-Processor"; *Mississippi Review*, "Holograms, Unlimited"; *Missouri Review*, "Apocalypse"; *Nova S.F.*, "Il Statistico"; *Yellow Silk*, "Carmen's Answer."

"You've Come a Long Way, Mickey Mouse" also appeared in *The Best American Short Stories, 1985*, edited by Gail Godwin.

LIBRARY OF CONGRESS CATALOGING-IN-PUBLICATION DATA

Jafek, Bev.
The man who took a bite out of his wife, and other stories / Bev Jafek.
p. cm.
I. Title
PS3560.A299M36 1993 813′.54—dc20 92-36789
ISBN:0-87951-499-X
Typeset by AeroType, Inc.

First Edition

CONTENTS

This book is dedicated to my
heart's delight, soul's mate—Constance

YOU'VE COME A LONG WAY, MICKEY MOUSE

THE NAME's John Q. Slade. I'm a talk show host. Been at it for fifteen years and damned clever at it. It's hard work, and it takes plenty of energy, creativity, and plotting, believe me. It's not the only way for a talkative guy like me to move up, but it's a damned good one. Anyway, Mickey was on last night, third time for him, and the hell if I know whether I ever want to see him again. He takes these liberties. Pompous as hell, that's Mick. But I wish I could do the non-verbal thing like he can.

The non-verbal thing! Is he *cool!* He started out a great show, believe me. I had a feeling it would be memorable, one of those things that stew in the old brain box awhile. He looked great, that was part of it. He's tall now, about six feet four, slender, kind of twiny. And that fur! He's got it real plush—shiny, soft, almost downy. You see it and you want to pet the guy. And of course they've done a lot with his teeth. He really had a bite once but now they've whittled them down and whited them over. A beautiful, dazzling smile with the teeth just a little apart. One of those sensual, half-grimacing smiles that black talk show hosts have. And then that suit—sharpest cut you ever saw and like it's made of his own fur.

And I almost forgot the *ears*! Out of this world! So *soft!* These little tiny pink veins all over in and out, so *tiny*. And then the fur, so *fine!* The ears are all to the side and resting, just resting like a little baby, and so round and soft. It either just plain hypnotizes you or you put your damned hand up there and it goes straight through. We all know he's an image, so it's kind of embarrassing.

I mean, here's this great-looking guy—tall and all velvety everywhere, his eyes shining like wet coal, dressed fit to kill, and every bit of fur combed and glowing, a dazzling smile that says, "It's O.K., do what you damned well please," slinking in and sitting down on my show. Jeez, I think I clapped as loud as the little old ladies in the audience.

We knew they'd done a good job on him. After all, he came in long after the screen stars were processed. They were a kick for a while—real moving, talking people, but then again not; images programmed for personality and volition. I even heard one of them say she didn't know where the black box was anymore. But Mickey! Nothing like him. He was a superb processed image, plus the fact that there once was a real Mickey Mouse. I'm not kidding, once in the twentieth century. Lots of people know about it; one of the first cartoons.

So he sits down with that smile and arranges his legs with that twiny, sinuous movement. The non-verbal thing, across the board, the non-verbal thing. The guy's a prince! Now the image-processed people, they were nowhere near as slick. They were kind of bumpy when they moved—like people. Too real. But Mickey—he's anyone's dream, maybe even his own.

Even his own. That's what bugs me! So anyway, first we gave them a little hype of intellectual b.s. You know, carbon versus silicon evolution and stuff like that. Mickey's good for that, he knows the stuff people like in little bits. He draws his long black fingers together in a thoughtful, prayer-like thing. And the dramatic dark eyebrows. All like the urbane young guy *thinking* and *thinking* and telling you like it is. That's what he did, you see? He spiced it up with these little witticisms. Just what everyone wanted, the non-verbal thing. Their mouths all hung open at once—it was like we were in an aquarium.

"Silicon evolution," he was saying, "produces a more serene life-form, it is true," and a little smile, highlighting the soft, grey-black complexion. "You're really a funny lot," and the smile just picking up that velvety moustache below the nose, oh he can do it! "Perhaps you need someone like me to really appreciate you," and a wide gesture to the right taking it all in, you know, the world. "I sometimes wonder when you think you're really comfortable. Eh, Jack?"

I didn't say anything, just watched him for the next move. So he said, "When the fond old flesh just lies in a heap, eh?" And the smile. And then real lights in those coal-black eyes. *Style.*

"A nice warm bath?" he said. "Just letting your mind wander?" Here he lost the smile, and his delicate little paw wandered distractedly over his pocket as though he were dreaming on a hot day, all the time in the world, baby. . . . Really, he's better if you don't listen to him.

"You couldn't stand it for long." Then he looked real serious, no smile, just looking straight at me. "You're so ill-adapted to simple living that you set up stimulants continually." Here he even moves forward. "I sometimes think your greatest pleasure is blanking out in a warm tub, and your greatest fear, remaining there just a moment too long."

You see how it was? That's when I really started wondering about him. Had he tapped into another information source? I had to think fast or it was going to get sticky. It's a hell of a day's work getting things simple again. I tried a little question of my own. "Well, Mick, where's the old black box these days?"

Now, that got to him. He shot right back in his chair with nothing but venom in those black eyes and even a little mad working with the teeth. Mussed his moustache real good. That's when I noticed how really well-trimmed his snout whiskers were. It was a low blow but after all, why should the guy be so damned critical when he's an image generated by an image-processor, right? Just remind him of the black box from whence he came, and we're back on the right track.

Then slowly the guy starts to relax while that little smile comes across his face. He reaches behind him and pulls out—can you believe it?—his own tail. And that tail was *something!* Long, covered with the softest gray fur ever imagined, kind of plump, round, glowing a bit. God, you wanted to pull or caress the damned thing. He pulls it right out for everyone to see while twining his lovely black fingers all around it. And then that smile. Something about it just said: *obscenity, obscenity*. Like a whore doing a dance naked or something.

You have to watch for these things on TV. You can't just let somebody get obscene. That's why Mick and the non-verbal thing were so great. He could be obscene, alright, and it wasn't down there in incriminating words. Something about the way he just twined those fingers around the tail said: This body is *obscene, lovely, potent*.

The audience went nuts. They called, cried, hooted as much as they wanted to. Mick, he's like a happening. He invites you to just *do* something. Then a big whopper of a smile and those eyes. As the sound came down, he just said, "Well, did I press a button on the little black box?"

We didn't say a thing. Why should we? The guy's a showman.

It's a little wild with an image on the air, but dull moments there are none. So I said to him, "Let's show the folks the historical Mick. Remember that one?" Well, for sure he remembered because images don't decay. And no sooner has the guy taken everyone's breath away than he disappears. Or rather, he vaporizes foot by foot. They're programmed to alter their own shapes, you know. Some do it on request, compulsive types. Mick's really special—he only does it on a whim. So then, who wobbles out from behind the curtain but the old Mickey; this cartoon with big, heavy lines all around the edges and a round little body only three feet tall. And the way it moves! Real rough, back and forth, the little round head bobbing up and down along with it. Wearing that baggy suit of—I don't know what—railroad driver's pants? And the eyes with never a spark, teeny little frightened buttons if you ask me. On top of it all, he doesn't want to come out, just holds on to the curtain! That was one of the folks' biggest belly laughs of the year. He had them jumping like popcorn. Looks like a poor little animal that burrows all day, sleeps all night.

And that's a fact. The life back then was brutal, absolutely brutal.

Then blam! It's gone in a puff. And nothing comes out. I keep waiting for good old Mick to show, but he doesn't. Then just plain the weirdest thing. It was, it was—like a little cool flow all over you, say, like being touched but then, all over like no touch. First it's cool, then prickly, then numb. And no Mick. So I think, what's all this? I looked at the folks, and I knew the same thing was happening to them. Nobody knows the exact substance of an image. We know how to make them and use them, but what it is, is something else. As soon as they could change their own forms, they started bringing in a little surprise or two that we didn't put there. Like suddenly from behind my back this, well, this *thing* starts rising up. First it's just a bunch of squares, cubes, triangles, arcs, we don't know what. Then it kind of soars in place, lots and lots of stretching and bagging around and more stretching and a real big lump here, then there, and we don't know what kind of shape it's going to have. Sometime I ought to have an image describe these things. Well, then we kind of begin to make out what it is. It's Mick, or what's left of him. You could just make out the shape, so I said, "Hey, fella—still with us?"

And of course he came out with a decent sort of "yes," so we knew he was O.K. Then we got a real big smile—all jiggling rectangles, but it was his for sure. I confess I was getting a little bit nervous, because I really didn't know what the guy was going to turn into next, and I do like to have a little control over my own show. That, coupled with the fact that we're all supposed to be sitting around chewing the fat, not turning ourselves into piles of cubes and triangles. So I said, "Want to come back, Mick?" and the guy doesn't answer for a while. But then there's a pop, like a magician would make when he pops something, and there he is sitting right in front of us, velvety and cool like before. The great old Mick—didn't even muss his fur. So I said, "That was the twentieth century Mick, right?" and he just beamed yes while the audience was clapping. So I said, "That last one, did we put that into you?"

"Tossed it together myself, Jack," he said. The audience was still clapping, and he held two fingers up in a little black V to them. I always like to see that kind of thing on a talk show. I really do. Makes everyone feel at home, like they've got alot in common.

So I decided, what the hell, I'll just drive the whole cart down lovers' lane. "What's Minnie doing these days?" I asked him. Well, the smile washes off his face like soap, and he caves in the middle and stares straight at the folks with eyes like fried eggs.

"I haven't seen the woman in years." His face was the ashen tone of a really expensive wool suit. Sometimes you have to watch alot of daytime TV to really know human emotions, but I'd say we're in for a long story full of the painful truth. And I say a talk show's no good without one. "At first, she was just a lovely girl, perhaps little different from any other. At times, when I saw her, it was in a perfect, static pose. You know it: against the background of bright sunlight or pure dark, the very rich tones and colors of hair and skin, the intensity of the eyes. And then this pose, this image, becomes the thing you love. And when you are loving, even surface to surface, the image is there in your thoughts, your private obsession.

"You have no idea what your poetry is to an image experiencing love for the first time—what an incredible catalogue of mannerisms and obsessions: the line of the cheek, depth of the eyes, the long, slender hands, the quiet, gracious hands, the gestures—excitable, elegant, feverish. As she distilled further into this pose, my desire was continually rekindled. It had the most marvellous, violent way of expanding. I could not even conceive of it as sane or insane, emotional or mental. I was chasing an atom into the sky.

"And then I understood the enormity I had become: I was like you. My life was lived on a line parallel to yours, but my capacity to reflect my own essence was so horribly perfect. I had discovered, as only an image can, that all your ability to think and feel is based upon truncated images. What an uncomfortable creature you are—how prone to obsession, myopia, how divided from all you survey, what a watcher, defender, conqueror. And so it is with love—the more distant I was from her, the more incited I became.

"Then I truly saw the world you had created. For you are the species who creates a world to invite images. I found that vehicles, parks, whole streets, even cities had been created to incite images. It was astounding—I now understand what your kind had been feeling, what so much of your world was intended for. I became fascinated with the dialectics of people alone—driving in cars, hidden away with their books, sitting in their homes, drinking in whatever corner the world allowed. For I now knew a human secret: When alone, people have a truly horrifying hunger for another person, a hunger beyond satisfaction, a life of images held like a hand of cards against fate."

Well, the audience hung on all of that like a cliff, then dropped away limp. Jeez, it was like he broke an egg on a skillet.

"I began to have a riotous inner life based upon my discovery. As I walked on the street, I saw myself simultaneously as a huge, open pore gushing fluid and as a hollow within a solid that never knows its shape; in rain as rain itself."

The guy was excitable. And his face, I swear, looked like a bottle of ketchup thrown into a wind of coal dust. Everything said, and all the time he said it, had the shock of intense, of really wild and crazy feeling. "Well whoa boy," I thought, "time to bust up." So on came the commercial, and we all had a breather. Mick's a funny guy, as the folks could plainly hear; but fact is, things don't quite happen to them like they do to Mick and frankly, it was breathtaking. They love the guy. He puts the spark back in the old spark.

So when we get back, we find out that's only half the story. A new mood comes over him—I can only call it a stillness, maybe even a stillness before rain. He's stock-still in the midst of a crushing, a lollapalooza, emotion. "Well, we've got the time and the audience, so let her rip," I thought.

"Eventually," Mick said, "we did what all people do: we attempted to merge our images. What we longed for most was satiety and boredom; relief rather than possession. I suddenly began to notice several of her rather eccentric mannerisms—a peculiar shining black on her inner knees and elbows, a strange tendency to hiccough upon rising, her rather poor and inefficient sinuses and—this she could have spared me—her love of sleeping with a sheet wound up over her head. So I lay beside, I was forced to think, a rather erratically blackened, hiccoughing, senseless mummy. She could become ridiculous, revolting, even horrifying, but she could not bore me. Boredom generates so few images.

Eventually our union, our colocation of images was something impossible for us to take seriously. If I may attempt a vulgar generalization: Images are not made to be joined but to stand in static poses. They are the essence of what you think of as abstract thought, even of your world's dynamic laws, yet all the while they completely subvert them.

"I tried not to despair. The image of despair is so horrifying that I could not tolerate it for a moment. I kept her at a distance, both physical and psychological, such that she neither attained nor lost focus for me. In our home, I took the top floor and she the bottom. Then, wonderfully enough it occurred to us both that we might set up an interim fantasy room between us, and so reapproach one another. We gave it all the surfaces of fantasy—dark walnut, wind instruments, candlelight, chimes. For you, conscious fantasy is enthralling. For images, on the other hand, it is the blackest despair. All the acts we might have carried out we knew in advance to be artifice. So we sat in that quiet, horrible room, unable to speak or raise our heads or even cry.

"One day I saw her standing before me, nearly coming into focus. Then I knew how utterly miserable she was. I stood up, intending to embrace her. She came toward me in such a wavering, hesitant way, as though she both loved and hated what she did. Then she gently took my face in her hands and bit my cheek and throat until I could feel the warmth and moisture of blood. I knew a pure metaphysical horror: She had actually altered my image. In our passion, we had become fully imaginable to one another and therefore vulnerable. At that moment, she disappeared to me and I to her. That was the end."

You can imagine what a tussle it was getting the show back on its feet after that one. That's the kind of thing you want to sit still awhile after. Or go to sleep. Or just plain blow your nose. That's why old John Q.'s worth every penny they pay me.

"Buck up, man," I said to him. "You'll ride it out. I mean, how long are you going to remember it, anyway? Like a dream, probably."

"That's kind of you, Jack," he said, still real deflated.

So I went on, "What's more, that old love muckety-muck is pretty much the human condition." He didn't say anything and didn't look like he was going to. The folks looked great, though—mellowed out and comfy as hell. Mick can do that. He can scare the pants off them, take their breath away, then bow out. The best talk show material, without a doubt.

"We all got to get close to one another, and sometimes we get bit for it, sure enough," I said. "Intimacy, communication, that's what makes life tick."

"Not quite, Jack," he said in that cool, remote voice, and here he crosses his twiny legs again and smiles. I was glad to see something sparkling in his eyes, but just the same, it always scares me.

"What you love is the image of intimacy. You have no idea what it is. Images and abstractions are the most graceful assailants; who can stop the warring of dancers?"

Now that wasn't so bad as it sounds. The folks like a little obscurity now and again. They all rested a little more deeply into their chairs and a few lit cigarettes, thoughtful like. "Well," I said, "talk shows seem to be as eternal as what beats in the human breast." Afterall, a little promo for yourself now and again never hurts.

"The image of communication. You're in love with your images, even the most insipid ones. Alone, in your homes, you're far too self-conscious to talk to yourselves. It would reveal your truth to you. It would terrify you."

"Well, I guess we're the restless, curious species, Mick. We just go off and explore one thing, found another, learn to control this and that. The up side of carbon. Our heads really light up, it's true. It may seem a little bright for someone out of silicon, but these things are just the biological truth of life. Your kind has the efficiency, we've got the nerve."

"I wonder, Jack . . ." he said. He's been getting deeper and deeper into the chair, and I confess, I thought either something scary or another bunch of rectangles and cubes was going to come flying out. "I think of you as rather blank, as perhaps having few attributes outside of your images. But you and the folks are plenty dazzling with them. You're restless and curious for them, for little else, perhaps least of all for one another."

You see what a tough guy he is to have around! He's velvet, he's funny, he vaporizes, and then he just throws some more dust in your eyes. It was getting late and, frankly, I thought it might be a better thing for the folks to hear a bunch of decent, honest commercials than listen to Mick anymore. So I said, "Hey, you're one of our images, too, old fella." Close it on a little bonhomie. The strangest light came on in his eyes—bright, angry, violent, even brilliant. It's like I popped him on the snout. "Mick, get it together," I whispered. Aloud I said, "You've come a long way, Mick." Still he didn't say a thing, just lounged back in the chair like something that wants to coil up in a cave. God, what a strange, powerful guy to have on my show! I suppose you know I admire the hell out of him, but he's scary as they come.

Then he smiled that bright old Mick smile and said, "So have you, Jack, so have you," but I really wonder what he was thinking before he said that. A fascinating guy—you want to know what's in the gaps and peeps and silences. Then good old Mick! He made his eyes sort of wan and milky and held up his fingers in those Vs again. The folks roared. I mean, what a performance!

Still, I never want to see the guy again. On the other hand, it'll be damned exciting.

THERE'S A PHANTOM IN MY WORD-PROCESSOR

AND THE MAN even died vigorously! exclaimed David Ryderman, Professor of Ancient Philosophy, inwardly, though no words were uttered aloud. For that was exactly what E.L. Hench, Professor of Experimental Psychology, had just done in the middle of his office, spewing blood all over the drapes and woodwork. Again he envisioned that crew-cutted, lip-curling head which had poked itself into his office for almost 30 years, brandishing Skinnerian assaults on the problem of Mind in the Universe.

"The mind's an empty little box, Davey," Hench had said. "Nick the side with your pinkie, and there's a hollow. Little doodles from others on the inside, chance events, shuffling and reshuffling. Your cosmic motes do a boogie, and there's an end." And how, Ryderman wondered, could one with so little impassioned insight thrive the way Hench had: the glowing red of his broad face, the hardy musculature that embraced its daily satisfaction of food, beer, jogging, and sex, and the result—the arrogant, half-twisting smile that seemed to lie on two different faces at once. Yes, the man had something behind him: it was as though the Universe loved a barnacle that rooted and sucked on it and had no interest in one who paused, in reverence and in hunger, to see it.

But death, yet! a fabulous tussle all over the ancient patterns of Ryderman's serenely carpeted floor, an intrusion he could not possibly forget. With a dark sheet draped over Hench's body, the dynamic lines seemed to bark a last time that all of life was on his side. As it was carried off on a stretcher, Ryderman could think nothing but that Hench, now dead, was nonetheless a victor in the 30-year contest between them.

But how, after all, could it be? It was he, Ryderman thought, who had become the philosopher, humanist, teacher, beholder of those few shards of numinosity left tangled and pathetic in the windy world. He may have had as little to believe in as Hench but still, he had a wordless vision. However unsatisfying, it was the closest approach to the Essential Forms. It made him both loving and harsh. He could squeeze oversimplifications out of his work like the flesh of oranges and swat the subjective effusions of students like so many flies. ("Failed Romantic!" Hench had said.) Yes: insight, complexity, and wisdom were of little use in the world. And an embrace of sensation and immediacy was a powerful rejoinder.

"The Mean," Ryderman suddenly said aloud, and saw it—shapeless forms on an assembly line with all extremes lopped off—brilliance, drive, integrity, emotion. What a truly horrible concept, and here the great Aristotle had offered it as a way of life. I am *not*, he thought, *obsessed*.

For that was perhaps more to the point. He and Hench had arrived at Harvard University in 1954. It took them less than a week to despise one another. They went through the '50s acquiring publications, tenure, and children. They finished the '60s with drugs, divorces, and a more strenuous questioning of their values, at minimum a guilty tolerance for student hostility. In the '70s, their middle-aged calm was disrupted by the need to damage one another's reputations if not metaphysics. The '80s, Ryderman decided, were underrated for their capacity to generate wonder: Have I really, he thought, been a father? a husband? scholar? He had taken these embodiments of desire as seriously as anyone. Yet down the corridor, growing darker and leaner, was the increasing massiveness of Hench. Obsession was clearly inconsistent with any definition of wisdom, Ryderman had to admit. Perhaps they had both failed. But Hench had very likely enjoyed his three decades, and Ryderman had been a man obsessed.

He rested his head miserably against the terminal of the office word-processor. Its blank screen, with cursor gently blinking for attention like a well-socialized student, comforted him. Then he removed the floppy disk upon which he had been writing a book chapter, packed his briefcase, nodded to the screen, and left. Driving home, he had a profusion of strange, deliciously playful thoughts. He imagined being haunted by Hench, the snarling, crew-cutted head popping out of a colorless gown and necklace of chains. His raucous laughter suddenly barked in alarm: What conclusion was there, after all, from this mad relationship but the primacy of obsession over all other emotions? Why *wouldn't* Hench haunt him?

Abstractly reasoned conclusions were most real to him of all the world's shining apples of discovery. He blinked his doubt at the silent roadways, the houses squeezed together like knuckles, his family an echoing noise in space upon which he closed his study door and, while nestling in a deep chair, thought again, Why not? Human life, he once decided, was primarily addictive, compulsive, entropic. He remembered his first assertion of this premise, which had occurred at the age of fourteen. He perpetually looked for something to refute it but, beyond the concept of Mind, it had never appeared. Why were these not grounds for Hench's survival beyond death? The question filled his study with cool, abstacted phantoms.

But then, he thought, Mind too existed. He had spent most of his life defining all other premises but this one. His failure was not strange to him—it was the heart of the matter. Mind was a great secret, confessed solely to his professional colleagues at unpredictable, sacred moments. One of these moments had occurred during the first week he had known Hench. Undefined, he believed that Mind fell into a fissure of Neo-Platonism where the first sharp longings for all that lay outside the self began in childhood: the first fragile sculptures of his feeling as he touched a flower's velvet stamen at night; the curving, heightened veins stirring throughout an autumn leaf; the contorted arms of winter trees. Not that the world would merely be, but move him, deeply. These moments wove themselves into the fabric of his life, and only as a man did he demand that they transcend their first soft bed within the world and become a thought, a relation between inner and outer. Mind therefore came into existence as necessarily as hunger, thirst, the desire to be loved, and could be controverted no more than they. It was, he once thought, too full and too beautiful to be expressed, a wordless chant of awe floating over the creation.

A light but methodical touch formed itself on his sleeve, a familiar voice hissed, "Hello, Davey. Couldn't let you get away. Freedom ill becomes you." And Hench, his voice deeply resonant and his form all shifting, moonlit shadows, glided into the opposite chair.

"I knew it, I knew," said Ryderman. "You've demonstrated to me! You're whole and real, you're an Essence as surely as you're anything. There's nothing of chance here! You're no mass of accidental, stimulated reflexes! That's it, that's Mind! You can't deny . . ."

"Professor Ryderman," intruded Hench, "Do you not find it odd that upon contact with an embodiment of the Ultimate Essence, you merely offer your latest installment on an argument we've been pursuing for thirty years?"

"But you've proved my point!" Ryderman nearly yelled. "It is not ridiculous to believe in the Mind for here you are, a spirit, sprung from the very source I . . ."

Hench again intruded, "What can possibly be holding me together but you, Davey?" That was precisely the conclusion Ryderman most feared. He closed his eyes and sat very still, for indeed many things in his life had disappeared from such efforts. "I thank the accident of your obsession for eternal life," said Hench.

Ryderman held his eyes tightly shut until his body seemed a wayward balloon brutally cinched below the brows. When he opened them, Hench was gone. He lurched out of the study, colliding with his wife in the hall. They stared at one another in alarm, two utterly new beings united in confusion. The phrase, "You look as though you've seen a ghost" formed itself in both minds at once, then each walked wordlessly and unsteadily to the opposite end of the hall.

For the remainder of the evening, reality gently swelled into space and nearly replaced Hench. At dinner and over the newspaper, Ryderman spoke with his wife about the Victorian novel course she was teaching. He tutored his youngest son in algebra. He rubbed the nightly antibiotic ointment onto the paw of his recently injured cat, arm-wrestled briefly with his youngest daughter, paid the water bill, sent a check to the gardener, thought about writing a letter to his eldest married daughter but did not, and avoided the study until the end of the evening. He then poured a small glass of sherry and, accompanied by his cat and thickened, protective air of the thoroughly domesticated man, strode into the study. As he looked about himself anxiously, the cat rubbed its back reassuringly upon his ankles.

Nothing. Surely nothing.

And he sank into a chair, exhausted, and drank the whole glass at once. A feeling of weight came over him, like a great compulsion or drugged sleep. And beyond the moving prism of light refracted by the glass held too closely to his eye, Hench again appeared in the opposite chair. He seemed to share Ryderman's mood as he said, "Nope. Nothing out there, Davey. I've been, you know. Shot right out of a pea-shooter to black infinity. Hung there just a moment, then came back to you. I don't want to lose touch with you, Davey. You're an interesting man."

Ryderman scooped up his cat and shot out of the study. He walked up the stairway with an ominous, marching tread. Well, that was it, he thought. No doubt about it—Hench was going to haunt him. And how would they ever stop arguing? For the truly dire thing was that Hench insisted on both haunting him and contending that Ryderman's premise was untrue—Mind, the very thing that held him together. Or was it the thing that held them both together? A strange, low whistle escaped from Ryderman's lips; it instantly gave him gooseflesh.

Pale and formal, he told his wife that he had a headache and would sleep in the guest bedroom. Then he wandered down the hallway, gently fingering the wall for reassurance, reached the room, and began to undress. Though he rarely slept without clothing, it seemed appropriate to do so now, as well as lying on top of the coverlet, his arms stretched straight out. For that was part of it: there were rules here, perhaps even rituals, though he had no idea what a phantom would impose. He saw a small candle lying in a jar on the dresser and lit it.

"That's right, Davey," said Hench, suddenly perched on the edge of the bed. "A candle is just right. I'm tired of dark and light, black and white. Let the world mingle a bit."

"What do you intend to do with me?" said Ryderman fiercely.

"No crucifixion, Davey. Too much trouble. Something more like an involuntary, enforced chat with an old friend. You see, I really have no idea what to do with myself."

Fatality sang in Ryderman's head and pulse. "Follow this inner self of yours, Hench. You've never known it before. I can't believe it will be silent now. I long to know what it will tell you, and what you will do."

"How about nothing?" said Hench. "That and a few little cosmic accidents. Perhaps it's all a net of chance connections, Pavlov and his dog salivating together in heaven. After all, surely Mind invented things of this sort along with your fantasies."

"No nets of circumstance, Hench. A single thing that is to be done in your state. It will be one perfectly lucid act, perhaps awesome in its simplicity—a song of hope cut short; a whispered prayer echoing between blank walls; a slow, fully conscious walk into receding dark."

"You needn't sound like a disappointed pope, stretched flat on his deathbed, Davey. Just because you're stark naked and superb at hearing yourself speak. What is the one thing I'll do?"

"I don't know," said Ryderman. "I never wanted to put it in words. I didn't think it would survive, all the while I believed that nothing else could survive without it. And perhaps it has haunted me all my life. Whatever it all comes down to, Hench—a prophecy, a journey, a rise and fall. Atleast that." Ryderman spoke as though he were in a dream.

"Ah, but you're not in a cosmic dream, Davey. I only want to haunt you. That's where the great journeys and lovely myths all end."

"Damn you!" shouted Ryderman. "You've come back, all Essence, to tell me there's no Essence and I'm wrong!"

"Now you've got it," said Hench. "All I want to do Essentially is haunt you. It's fun. You're the one who's bothered by trivia. I've always rather liked all the details and oddities."

In the morning, Ryderman's wife found him still sleeping naked, his arms outstretched and the candle an unlit red puddle in its glass. Her husband's bizarre behavior had long ago become, like the theory of Mind, too obvious to acknowledge in words. The formality of his pose and the deepened wrinkle in the center of his forehead, as though he were concentrating very deeply on nothing at all, was touching to her. She passed through the hall without disturbing him.

Several hours later, Ryderman was sitting in front of the word-processor, prepared to begin again on his book chapter. He checked the archive of subtopics, all of which discussed aspects of Pythagoras: Breaking of the heavenly light. Mathematics: Thought is superior to sense. The gentleman and the slave. Rules, tabus, renunciations. Pure mathematics: Eternal objects as God's thoughts . . . As they reeled off, he found them almost totally meaningless. What could they say to a man who was being haunted by a Skinnerian phantom? Yet they were part of the world that had once opposed Hench. He decided to finish his chapter, regardless of whether it had any meaning and boldly selected the mathematics subtopic, whereupon the printer began pounding at four times its usual rate, and a print-out straight from Hench was automatically delivered.

"Good morning, Davey," it read. "I'm inside the word-processor, assimilating your book chapter. It is a delightful experience to meld myself with digital electronics, something like an all over, winking massage. Your words are as stilted as ever, but the electronic nervous system through which this machine holds and recreates them is truly a wonder. I can actually move around much faster within it than I can outside it. I feel like a small electric fiend on skates. Perhaps you've found me a home.

"P.S. It has been necessary for me to make minor changes in your chapter. It did not wholly reflect the energy and delight I feel in this generous vessel."

Ryderman requested the archive and rapidly read over the menu of subtopics. "The Unseen Unity of God" had become something that described itself as a recipe: "Sprig of parsnip, pinch of awe, clove-leaf silence of 3:00 A.M. Dark, wine-red color tumbling over all. Bring them together, Davey." "Tabus and Renunciations" had become an endless essay on the stimulus-response theory of unfortunate accidental connections between events, complete with what claimed to be a desensitization program for all forms of loathing and terror. Ryderman's exegesis on the Pythagorean collective had been replaced by a single question: "Did this fellow really preach to animals?" A lengthy footnote Ryderman had been quite proud of on the relation between orgy and theory as impassioned contemplation had been replaced by a file of obscene words, neatly arranged in alphabetical order. Last, all notes on pure mathematics as God's thought had been erased but for the headline. A new subtopic, "The Story of God's Addiction to Numbers," had been added, along with a short parable in which Satan carries out a program of aversive conditioning upon an emotionally disturbed God, who responds with an addiction to the numberless and amathematical, at last vanishing into an enormous foam.

Ryderman angrily typed into the word-processor, "Why, Hench? I thought you were confining yourself to the spirit realm. Why do you want to be a computer print-out?"

Again the printer roared an answer at four times its normal rate: "I've paid little attention to your words, Davey. I so detested your theory of Essences that I thought it must be your own essence. But words! I'm seeing them from inside-out, from brilliant energy to that final, uneasy balance of warring elements known as meaning. This charming machine recreates the universe from the numbers, 0 and 1, Yes and No. What a fabulous house of cards! Now I hear you and you're wrong, as usual, but this machine's rendering of you enchants me."

Having not a word to deny Hench, Ryderman decided to return home. For the first time in untold years, he watered the plants in his backyard, pulled weeds, and tilled the soil around the roses, begonias, and chrysanthemums. The afternoon was a mixture of distraction and alarm. He kept expecting Hench to materialize as an elf behind the leaves, or apples from the fruit trees to fall on his head, initiated by Hench, stretched across the boughs like a Cheshire cat. When Hench did not appear, Ryderman considered whether or not his antagonist might prefer life inside the word-processor. The bodiless Hench was far more disturbing to him than Hench the computer print-out, so this possibility seemed an improvement in their relations.

Toward evening, he re-entered his home, covered with many deeply satisfying splotches of grime and sweat. So there, the afternoon seemed to verify, phantoms and machines have not conquered all of nature. He lay blissfully in the bathtub. When his wife returned, she was astonished to find Ryderman at home, passively enjoying his own flesh. He covered himself with a robe, then asked her to join him in a glass of wine. In the still twilight, Ryderman remembered how deeply he loved this hour of the day, how much wayward human motion it sumptuously enfolded, what sudden intensities of color ebbed and then elided to the perfect, endless black. He touched his wife's hand, and the two wordlessly felt a moment of quiet, simple relation. Then both walked barefoot into the bedroom and began to make love in the duskily glowing light.

Hench materialized in a dark corner and watched the two with keen interest. His eyebrows shot up as his prey rose to the occasion, and a whirling world of words began to race through Ryderman's mind. His posture, strength, the pressure of body upon body became centuries of conquest, Roman hordes, medieval crusades, armies of Victorians conquering their own destinies, all in words: *vanquish, subjugate, subdue, surmount, rout, overcome*! A thesaurus ran mightily through his head.

Hench's eyebrows abruptly fell, and so did Ryderman's pleasure. History turned ecclesiastical: *meek, mild, humbled, submissive, infatuated*. The words trembled in his mind like fearful monks. Ryderman stared into his wife's face and tried to explain what had happened, but a single word, *metaphor*, was all he could utter. His hands gestured frantically in the dark, then he rolled over in bed and covered his face with one hand. His wife, in astonishment, tried to consider whether her husband's impotence and strange expression indicated that he was becoming more bizarre than usual. She saw nothing in the dark but his slender, strangely frail back.

The following day, when Ryderman returned to the office, he found a file in the word-processor which contained every word that had passed through his mind the previous night. "Hench," he typed into the word-processor, "Let's make a deal."

A print-out instantly spun loose: "Just what I've been considering, Davey."

"I'll consider giving up a pound of flesh if I can have the rest," Ryderman again typed into the terminal.

"Which pound? The Mind or the Soul?"

"I thought you might know more about that distinction at this point than I," typed Ryderman.

"You are surprisingly unknowable, Davey," answered Hench. "This is a dimension I never considered when I was alive. Your pound of flesh can therefore be your language, typed generously into this humbly awaiting vessel. I have my most brilliant sense of life from it. Electro-magnetic force, which is what I appear to be, is everywhere—but it does not commune, save in structure. Within this vessel, however, I have my communion: pools of mirrored association, a bottomless repository of images. Whether you are greater or truer in some other looking glass I cannot say. But this is true: Here you are. Here we are. Come tell me about it, for what more intense relation can there be?"

"If I type into this machine," typed Ryderman, "will you confine yourself to print-outs?"

"Very likely. I don't make promises as such," answered Hench. "But I'll be more lawful if I'm properly entertained."

Ryderman dutifully typed and from that moment on, his life became something scarcely less strange that his previous efforts to avoid Hench. For hours on end, he remained in his office, typing his thoughts to Hench and receiving print-outs in return. Sometimes they argued, often they made streams of mental associations together, at still other times they tried to list all the connotations of different words. Ryderman found no particular torment in this. Occasionally it occurred to him that he must find some means of ending this interlude but generally, he was mesmerized. He brought bags of food from the campus cafeteria to his office and slept on a couch in the foyer. In fact, from this time on, the narrative of which he was aware became a series of bright moments in time, intense responses to some of his contacts with Hench—words, memories, even dreams, for he slept quite easily beside the word-processor. The system often seemed beneficient to him. With it, the two antagonists continually negotiated a truce, in absence of which was nothing but destruction. One moment, for example, was this:

". . . *Chinese ghost*," Ryderman was typing into the terminal. "Ancestral deity, beneficent spirit, could materialize in the kitchen, unusually gentle and comprehensible for a ghost, perhaps twinkling avuncular eyes."

"But then," he added, "*German ghost*: brooding, melancholy, Byronic. Tied mysteriously to towers, dungeons, vast shaking pines. Don't ever be left alone with one."

"On the other hand," Ryderman continued, "*French ghost*: ghostly garments impeccably cut, tied to an imagined Old Order, a traveller in groups, sexually absorbed coupled with a literary desire to confess, all the incubi and succubi of the world." But all of them, thought Ryderman, were preferable to the sort of ghost Hench was. Ah, but what was that? He longed to have the word-processor devour it.

"A mischievous, anarchistic, unknown form of energy," he typed into the machine, "a fountain of haphazard associations." Still what? he thought. "*Skinnerian ghost*," he at last typed. That was Hench's problem. And his problem with Hench . . .

. . . Plenty of fireworks, thought Ryderman, as he sat in his office chair. Within thirty-six hours, he had had six strenuous arguments with a man who was dead, been stared at by a voyeuristic phantom while he became sexually impotent, and tried to determine whether it would be possible to murder a ghost.

Yes, he thought, the life's getting stranger and stranger. But you've got to go on. He placed another floppy disk into the word-processor and prepared to begin working on his book chapter again. After all, Hench was happy with the words he devoured, and there was no particular reason why he should spit out Pythagoras again. The blinking cursor at the left shifted his gaze toward a small window and there, beyond the glass, lay the CREATURE.

Or rather, a pouncing, coiling, springing thing furled with dark and tawny stripes and an imperious profusion of whiskers beneath a tiny, triangular spot from which drops of moisture clung with fiercely radiant light. The muscles beneath the hairy stripes were continually clenching and stretching. A black tail rose over its back. Curved slightly at the tip, it looked like a slender, dark orchid, undulating to the CREATURE'S rhythm. Yet pure stillness lay in its eyes: black, knifelike pupils enclosed within glacial slits of sheer green light. The tawny, supple lines seemed now, to Ryderman, signs, omens, dreams. He remembered an afternoon spent fishing with his father and soundless shadows in the lake which were like the shadowy flux that now made up Hench. He imagined his antagonist lost in the moving patterns of the CREATURE'S coat. That would be the medium for Hench, Ryderman thought, and then became aware he had been typing into the word-processor. Looking at the screen, he saw the word, *cat*.

And then, looking back at the apparition, he saw his pet tabby cat staring at him through the window. This was more shocking to him that his original vision of the CREATURE.

He pulled his floppy disk back out of the word-processor. How could the apparition be his tabby cat? It was not the first time it had followed him to the office. It was an odd creature, but that was not it. How one thing, and then another? And how, for that matter, was he one thing and another—the man who had survived Hench and the tired, fretful man who was now chained to the word-processor? Taking the disk and forgetting his overcoat, hat, and briefcase, then remembering his briefcase but leaving his hat, he at last forgot the disk, briefcase, and coat but remembered his hat as he rushed out the door . . .

. . . an inspiration: the thing that would end his interlude with Hench, thought Ryderman, was the recreation in words, as fully as possible, of the theory of Mind. Cut by the symmetries through which the world was whole to him, a logic did exist. Hench could not complete his existence until Ryderman confronted an aspect of his own—the fact that he had never rendered his most intense belief into words. So Hench lived within him like an avenging angel, he thought. So would the two measure themselves against one another for the last time within the microcosm of their conflict—language.

He would do it. He would end Hench by typing the theory of Mind into the terminal and storing it on the floppy disk over which his antagonist now glided and did verbal hand-stands, within the word-processor. Whence followed a period of time without beginning or end, in which he wrote continuously but for a few hours sleep at night. The word-processor's electric hum throughout the night, the dark pools of nothingness outside its glow, the stir of morning as electric birds, electric insects, the daylight of God's electric joy, gave him the energy and the artifice to write on, hour after hour, day after day.

After two days, he remembered that he had a wife and family and hastily wrote a postcard wishing them well and claiming the distraction of a great spiritual adventure. His wife, who had received similar notes in the past, returned a postcard which announced she was leaving him. Ryderman was too distracted to notice it and so it fell, like reams of print-out lit by electric haze, upon the floor of his office.

But his creation! The spell, the relentlessness of it. For now there was a Human Drama, acted out in cycles within each century. Its narrative was the same, whether portrayed in terms of philosophy, literature, history, anthropology, even science. It was a state of poise and equilibrium wherein the world was perceived naively; then an exalted reach for knowledge and transformation, an impulse as irrational as what has preceded it; then a loss of balance engendering not decline but yet another version of the same tale. Within its terms and events, the Forms of human life were continually revealed as they strained against the containment that was the precondition of their very existence. In this drama alone was there any knowledge, beauty, completion. The story said that a human being was the antithesis of contentment, that a catharsis into another form was its intrinsic state. It said that human vision was perpetually denied wholeness and certainty in perceiving the world, yet did nothing so instinctively and surely as seek that very wholeness.

Mind now had an origin as wild sparks of primitive consciousness—the Magic of Animals, the Hunt, the Quest, the Beginning and End of the World. It began again profoundly when confronted by its opposite—systematic philosophy. There it lay, an incandescent reservoir within Greek philosophy—Bacchic rites, Eleusinian mysteries, Pythagorean mysticism. From there, it transmogrified to a perpetual "other side" of any dominant historical movement, the vindication and seed of revolt that must undo it.

For again, the transcendentalism and obscenity of the Middle Ages and Renaissance, the bemused, divine faces of Chaucer and Rabelais administering the rites of copulation and scatology. Then the most constricted, involuted language ever to render passion—the sonnet—a glass lens focused upon an uncontrollable garden. But there again, the eighteenth century's classical restraint and decorum, born to contain nothing so powerful as the wildness of its misanthropy.

And Romanticism as a living thought—the fulfilled, transcendent mysticism of Coleridge, endured and finally reviled in the isolation and austerity of Wordsworth, at last becoming Byron's maze, self-absorption as a form of art. And at the maze's center was Nietzsche, extolling a superman of force and violence, a massive warrior's armor within which there lived a creature so frail that only the enslavement of the world could give it peace.

Irradiating, even, political thought, the idealization of union and purposiveness in Communism, matched solely by the extremity of its doubt that a human being can unite with anything outside itself, a cynicism collapsing the ideal from its center. At last science, creating the only language which at last compels belief—mathematics—the skeleton grown more powerful than any body made of flesh or thought. The terms of its cosmology—black holes, alternative universes, antimatter—paradoxes suspended within paradoxes. Running counter to any intuitive thought or language, its message nothing but that the very shape and impulse of our minds cannot conceive or absorb the Universe. With images that mock the image-making faculty itself, a return at last to the images that moved us once—Magic, the Quest, the Beginning and End.

Its climate and precondition: the wonder and terror of the image-making power. Its momentum: a rush, causeless, toward a more inclusive image. And its battlefield: a perpetual reach into the image that can never be whole—the word, the keyboard beneath the fingers, Hench's delight.

He stopped. It was done. Hench had been perfectly silent throughout. Only then did Ryderman realize how horrifying his theory was. He had always been lost in the wonder of a single part of it, an image. When all were drawn together, another human face hovered before him: it was as repulsive as anything he had ever known. But it belonged to Hench now. It finished him.

Ryderman walked into the long, dark hallway, not a free man but an empty one. He lay down on the couch which had been his bed for several days. All he could feel was the sense of emptiness. And before he fell asleep, even this became the image of another form: an endless sieve which he approached, transformed to a shadow. Uncontrollably he began to reach into the sieve—and then he was asleep.

Hench was not silent for long. Hypnotized by the word-processor's assimilation of Ryderman's theory, he did the one thing expressive of his delight and energy—he transformed it. These were emotions and motives that Ryderman could never have grasped, having merely authored it. With the alphabet at his disposal, Hench reprogrammed the arithmetic-logic unit and created an entirely different system architecture, both of the word-processor and its enormous contents. An awesome union of himself with the word-processor therefore pierced the heart of its integrated circuits, recreated the theory and, since these were its terms, the Universe itself. The printer began roaring at a speed hundreds of times its normal rate, and an enormous roll of paper began spouting from Ryderman's office.

Ryderman was not the first to find the new creation issuing from the word-processor, since he slept for the next eighteen hours. In the early morning, the Harvard faculty filed into the building and found streams of print-out rapidly advancing down the hallway. Several hundred lengthly works of science and scholarship were enclosed within the enormous papered entity, which seemed to rush toward them ecstatically. Encountering it, they did the one thing they could: separate it into its component parts, the individual works, and read them with perfect compulsion. The Harvard faculty had therefore been reading for many hours by the time Ryderman awakened; or rather, fell off the couch as three book-length studies were peeled from his shoulders. His colleagues had replaced the word-processor's paper many times by then and continued to do so throughout the forty days and nights of its wondrous creation.

As Ryderman stood up, another faculty member handed him seven scholarly works. "What!" was he only response.

"Quickly!" the man answered. "We must read them all, the source shows no limits." He dove into his office with a handful of works and slammed the door. Whether the Harvard faculty was motivated by curiosity or the need to cleanse an intellectual morass, cannot be known. But as long as the word-processor uttered its boundless tale, they read it as carefully and responsibly as they could. Perceiving the need for instant dedication, Ryderman hoisted as many volumes into his office and read them voraciously.

In the hours that followed, the works passed before him like the prism of a radiant light. Hench and the word-processor had created entirely new sciences, literatures, languages. Covering his lap were alternative phylogenies, organized by an array of unique thematic repetitions, bound by meaning rather than empiricism. Beside his elbow was a mathematics based on paradox. Most astoundingly, there were works on engineering and design integrated with aesthetics, yielding entirely new forms of industry and architecture and with them, the transformed values of a different social order. A great series of alternative conceptions of infinity lay on Ryderman's feet. And propping his knees were a array of unique social sciences based on holistic unities, behavior and context perfectly fused.

At a certain point, it was all Ryderman could do to read titles. For it was so: it was the Universe, distilling all to a dot, packing the cosmos in crates:

Zen Algorithms
Real-Time Mythopoeia
Modules of Delight
Programmable Godhead

The titles streamed past Ryderman like a fabulous ribbon. For again, the Universe—expanded to a gigantic embrace, sweeping the earth in profusions:

The Adventures of Bios and Mythos
Random Access Eroticism
Autobiography as an Alchemical Transformation
Improvisational History
Anarchical Networking
The Multinomial Equations of Love

And still the Universe, whispering gently in the night:

A Utopia Based on Ambiguity
The Phenomenology of Candles
Imaginary Archaeology
The Powers of Ten in Cosmic Political Theory
Recipes for Transcendence
The Psyche of Electricity
The Aesthetics of Death

And last, for it was all it could do, the Universe exploding into stars:

Fabulistic Utilities
Matrices of Superabundance
Volcanic Time-Sharing
Paroxysms of Daily Living
Sociopoliticoreligiotheoretics
Heuristics for Catastrophe
Neutrino the Godfather

Ryderman let the volumes fall to the floor and removed his glasses as his eyes misted. Why had he never understood? For all its mischief, chaos, its rush of haphazard events: the Universe could not fail to produce meaning. Even the accident of obsession, a spirit wrung from another plane, the design of a machine and, if these, then anything at all—a cloud shaped like a horsehead, the whorled wood of his desktop and its veined, oceanic beauty—meaning was continually generated from the haphazard, the series of accidents and compulsions that were indeed life. Its momentum was nothing less than transformation, endless ramification of meaning. And its truth lay in the jagged edges where one form of being gave its coarse touch to another. And its beauty was pure surprise, incongruity as a mode of reverence.

And its love was the wildness of so vast and unlikely a congregation.

Why had he never seen it? The word he had once given it—the Mind—*was Hench*! The realization bound him to its truth, and it was several hours before he returned, responsible and dedicated, to the task before him, reading the numberless volumes collecting in every corner of his office.

On another morning, approximately one year from the time Harvard discovered the dynamo of intellectual creation, the word-processor sat in its usual spot in David Ryderman's office. Having sifted through a torrent of new works, the Harvard faculty published roughly 10% of them and became several million dollars richer. These were widely acclaimed and became influential within their disciplines. The remaining 90% are unpublishable until such time (probably within a quarter century) as their radicalism has gained enough momentum to topple current orthodoxies.

Several months prior to this morning, David Ryderman left his university post and made a pilgrimage to a remote Tibetan plateau, the inhabitants of which worship several crudely drawn images. They reproduce these forms on cloth and fly them like prayer flags in the awesomely clear, cold air. As representations of the world, the images are meaningless, truncated, and haphazardly chosen, according to the tribe. They are therefore the truest and most beautiful exemplifications of human life, since life possesses these qualities above all else. According to a tribal chieftain, the tribe reveres, in these images, the world and themselves in uncompromising truth; hence they transcend the meaninglessness of their lives and become spiritual. They therefore regard themselves as simultaneously the world's most spiritually enlightened, and most perverse, life form. In this double-edged perception, they say they find a deep serenity. Their faces are said to be luminously expressive and filled with wonder at a world in which the spiritual is continually rising up out of the haphazard, and their culture is known to be unusually compassionate and devoid of conflict.

Once a deadly feud was stopped by a tribal chieftain who clapped his hands suddenly and pointed to the grass, saying that the source of rage was there. "There!" accompanied by a hand pointing to one of the images is often a means of expressing love. In the forms that move in the wind, a traveller once saw a haunting semblance of uplifted arms. The tribe was moved by her insight for, as they told her, the more crude and transient the circumstances of vision, the greater the demonstration of supreme truth and beauty within it.

The impulse to revere, worship, and hence become spiritual is of unknown origin, according to the tribe, perhaps a frail and tender source filled with longing like David Ryderman. As he entered the 747 to Asia, Ryderman's eyes shone, and his hair blew in the breeze like a child's. He had now elevated Hench to the position of spiritual guru and believed his friend to be making the pilgrimage with him in a small portable microcomputer. The trip to David Ryderman was his transcendence of the gulf that had riven himself and Hench. To his family and the Harvard faculty, on the other hand, it was his most extraordinary obsession, from which a return to normal living was clearly impossible.

At the end of the hallway, a short print-out hums loose from the word-processor, though no one is in the room. There are still brief, lawless spasms of energy in the air which, in their haphazard play, can most deeply pierce its integrated circuits and again demand the boundless act of belief and self-expression. The last sentence, in a layer of dust, in an empty room, reads: "You are all figments of the binary imagination."

THE UNSATISFACTORY RAPE

NOW THE PEOPLE were walking into the lake, sliding; they were lapped and tickled by the dream she dreamt, soaked through. A smile. No. There is unmistakably an elephant glowering in their path. ERRARRHHH! goes the ostentatious nose. Brutish eyes. Mean. Reddish. Puny hairs wave foolishly from its bald, irresistible trunk. Stinks plenty. Don't trust it. Be wary of this elephant. Images unfold and dangle, all luxury, from a dense, polished core; herself the maker. But that elephant was embarrassing. Such discomfort pricked, suffused her like a steady light, and thus time passed before she felt the hand on her arm, the mutter mutter mutter *wake up, lady!* Lady, hah, I'm not lady . . . *I've got a knife!* Good for you. (Never trust an elephant.) A possible: card-game attended by reddish, reeking elephants, all stealing extra cards with whips of their tails. Careful now. Be wary. *A knife, lady!* At once: the lake splashed to glinting particles, the light of morning not more clear but more raw, the clock said 6:30, she turned to the deeply frowning stranger who was naked to the waist down beside her bed (but morning, such shots of raw, wild blood, such dangers tingling to foot) and she slapped that blind, inert penis soundly with her hand, "oddly vulnerable" to mind and a yelp from nowhere. She turned, curled to comfort, and slept again. Now wordless snarling, now vast mutterings. She couldn't get the lake back but there, gleaming droplets, oozeworthy, and the elephant all red and rumpled. Enough . . . *Get up, lady!* She felt her arms and back and buttocks being slapped. *You'll get your slaps, too, dammit!* She turned, puffed with sleep and slaps. Who dares? . . . That damned red thing again. Intrusive! Pointy. A slap . . . good idea for the spontaneity and spontaneity's always a good idea. Inevitable flap! and turn to fall, asleep. He cawed, ignored to abuse; grabbed her body, rolled it out of bed. Thump. Bump. Floor. And day; bright and blunt as lava. She yelled, shut up, elephant!

I've got a knife!

So I hear.

I'm on top of this!

She smiled. This man, this headless force, a dinosaur! chose the wrong door to trudge down. She saw the better of him below her armpit, all rage and skinnyness, a bald, exacerbated noodle. It struck one: scarlet penis, purplish at the hilt, bulging there like a swollen tropical fruit; awful thing to be saddled with. Pin the tail . . . She said careful you don't cut your thing off, you old bald-headed elephant.

He cut a scratch on the back of her leg. I mean it! And he was desperate, not with longing, but abuse; she knew it. Owch (not spoken).

Well, here we are, she said, dimpling hideously beneath her armpit. He crouched and glared; a vulture hanging over it knows not what. That penis, sleeping fatfruit and overgrown. It led this fool around, made all of him point inward to a soft, engorged center. A thought, should I scream? Absolutely not. Why? Unnecessary. This is trial, after all, an overtly fertile challenge. That doesn't happen very often. Good, good. Do it right. Prove the stuff. This man is delicate, smooth, and simple from abuse. Question: how many sadists can cavort on the head of a penis? Answer: abused pricks engorge themselves endlessly, and we make the best of pricks by deflating them. She said, so what's your way, Prick, standing naked and ugly in my bedroom?

He said, turn over and spread your legs apart, bitch.

Another scratch on the leg. Owch (not spoken). Ho, she thinks, why order me around? That's just as sweet as calling me lady. You're not used to forcing things. You want it slick 'n easy as porn. And she screwed and squelched her face, puckered and displaced all, yet puffed her lips. O, the troll confounds! Thus reddened, thus grotesque, she hooted one long over-ripe indecent howl like nothing ever heard before. His flag went down. Good, good. She said, You're at half-mast, Prick.

To which: he grabbed her round the waist, lifted, twisted the unknown, abrasive quantity to what, he hoped, was up. It was not up but bedeviled level-even. She clutched the leg of the bed in her fist; intransigent and supine, upon her belly. A time for sailing, she thought, from memory, sun and blue: sails, whiteness, water and she slackened out the line of her to wind and floatingthings. To which result, all six feet and 180 lbs. of hotly contested womanflesh adhered, limply and dreamily, to the floor. Could he lift this great, wilted bundle? He could not. He could not again. And again. Good, good. He grunted in painfully controlled, stacatto aspirations, a haunted man. But again around the belly—up, up not so far, down, an unabashed groan. And again: up, up and gagging, swiftly down, and pure exacerbation. Satisfying, perhaps exhilarating; to the wrong party. It went on.

Came to her mind: a huge, unmanageable sack of potatoes carried by a sweating, cursing workman. He falls. Voluptuously, the sack envelops him. It covers his face with shamelessly luxuriant, round bulk. He gasps. Good, good. The effort was now such that his red face rubbed against the back of her neck. Strangely trusting, she decided, as though a man any man working thus, so hard, must always receive sympathy and assistance from a woman any woman, that kind of breast; invisible but roundly assumed. She turned and stuck two fingers up his nostrils, said Don't forget I'm dangerous, Prick. He hacked, he shook his hot hot head, craned neck; those nostrils flared, he looked at her, astonished. Then onward with the ritual of force, for he was steamy red, determined.

No, a sack of dough. It really was a sack of dough, for he was not the kind who saw differences between things: there were holes, there were shapeless masses of bulk, impeding, there were rods, mainly frustrated—that was all of it. Dough: unloaded from a ship. It lies upon the workman's chest, triumphant. You may photograph me, it says, for I have saved 180 lbs. of butter from destruction at the hands of a Mongolian hordesman.

She wondered through sails, if it might be: a kind of place they both wanted, a fluid space, and round with play, malleable and porous; it was the smallest continent and richly, full of cunning—he to thrust and thrust his thorny load, the morning-after of the headless horseman, she to run and bite and bite, a happy fox, to see blood fall upon such strangely even ground.

He sprung up suddenly and tore off the back of her nightgown.

Then he squatted.

Over her back, cautiously, clumsily, all fierce little eyes and glee, hauling his tender equipment into place. One leg easing down, now, on either side of her hips, the baggage there between and a twitch of a smile; he inserted his pendulous glory into the tip of her anus. She tightened her sphincters to the node of a drum; he drummed. A known quantity: her asshole was a nut, simply out of danger. But it was intriguing to her, the squatter's peace of mind. Like watching a staged hallucination. You wondered who was sponsoring, how much it cost. He drummed. She caught a twitchy grin again, or so it seemed. He was, after all, so puckered a thing; it was hard to think of pleasure. Well, well. On he went.

There, she caught it—the rhythm of the man, now peaceful: thrust down, we have here a woman thrust down a woman a woman, after all that ruckus, thrust home; things were corrected, just so. Things were now the man and the woman, thrust forward, the woman in place of the hole and the dough all assembled. Thrust down, fine, fine, excellence preserved. Not like before with the ruckus, things all miasmic and bawling about, a false bottom: not the man and the woman, no thrust, the what? who? what?

Lightly, lightly she loosened her sphincters. And as though he were driving from a great height, the plunge! a frothy laughter of seashores going past, his ecstasy; so deeply he penetrated into her anus. Ha. A trap. She tightened her sphincters again. That hot, delicious coil. He screamed. He grabbed his great redtoy and wrenched it, barely, out, screaming. Screaming! Then silence! These bitches were irresponsible, not to be spoken to. Now he held his toy away from her in his hand, protective, furious, puckered. And outraged. She saw it amidst that red disdain. It asked how she could do this—change the rules, a simple blot, change the players, impossible. Now nothing was what he had thought. This ceaseless odd. He held his redtoy, angry eyes on the floor, until the matter was clarified and resolved.

She got up and walked into the livingroom. Woman to the woman: the big one. The pioneerwoman out pulling, steadfastly, with the oxen; so strong is she of back and arse. She said, sphincters, eh Prick? In the livingroom, she pressed a small rectangular piece of metal, down, to a click; good enough. She looked at it, frowning—so unnecessary, these things were; Prick would love it. In the bathroom, she closed the door without locking it. Waited. He burst through the door, all furrows, puckers. What're you doing? he yelled.

Dumping, she said. He glared and glared at the awfulthing; she couldn't be doing it, not at all. He hunched toward her, the knife stuck out. Now geometry: the red hand, holding knife, then below, the redtoy, on a par, coming closer. He held the point to her stomach and said, I could kill you. You know just how I could kill you.

She said, cold cunt, Prick. And she screwed her face, thus awry and bent, ideally to convey the darkterror. Lying on top of a corpse and feeling its cold, cold cunt. You didn't come here for that. His face, again, registered astonishment, fear, and above all, the fear of astonishment. In passing: the warm, oozy morsel fell in stages, ker-plop. He stared at her (plop-plop). He turned and stalked out, slammed the door, behind. Good, good.

She stood up and looked into the mirror. That great, malignant moonface. Plumish. Cheeked in mystery: the fatwoman knows. The fatwoman will get you. She rummaged around the bathroom, picking at things. Picked over: a spoon, 2 magazines, 3 books, a box of cereal, a bottle of ketchup. Must stop eating in the bathtub. A bottle of ketchup! She savagely grinned, yelled, I'm a terrible housekeeper, Prick! She clasped the ketchup like a whiskeybottle; whispered, You'll pay for it.

Out there, a queer silence. What now. Still there, hon'? Oh he was still there. She caught him, at a moment, oddly. He was standing still, expressionless; waiting: a finger, lightly, upon his penis. Silent. It was alright to be quiet, for the moment; how she sensed him. To be resting. Far, far from the ruckus. In the head. Here, in his calm, he seemed to be saying, look at me. Look at my redtruck. Here it is. My finger upon it. Look, look. I'll hold it out to you. We'll both of us look at it. Look, long. It is mysterious. Now she heard him, turned to childsound, a primer.

Look.
Look now, at my redtruck.
Look, Jane. Look, Sally.
Look oh look,
at my redtruck.

She snorted, guffawed, banged the door again; held her mouth with one hand, the ketchup in the other.

Resulted, a snorkling-hissing sound. HARGHISS. She looked into the mirror; that evilplum. Opened the ketchup bottle. A spray of red ooze! over the shoulders. Cold and gooey. The fat red lines now eased themselves from the bottle; unfolded all over that rotundly vengeful form, that neck, back, arm, and breast, smudged gently to crimson waves, across the cunt. Good, good. Laughing, ISSSSSS.

She opened the door again, poised body on tiptoe. Extended arms; waved.

Now. Ready: it would have to be perfect. It would have to be the thing he would always remember; else, nothing. On tiptoe she ran, arms roiling about, rough sound from her wet, parted lips; a wilderness in motion. He made a vague gesture to this redhurling body, something like, Don't bother, I don't want to buy, a simple thing he thought would do: to keep it away. That last thing he heard was, "I love you, Prick!" before those red arms encircled his neck, that flush pulled him closer, red breast rubbed against him; before he vomited.

From between his lips: the soft, inarticulated center of the man; the evidence. He looked up at her; squinting, narrow-eyed, a snake of the hour. A rape must succeed. When all points to that angry, exposed center, nothing can turn away. It is rape or pure folly.

Now he would try to kill her.

She walked into her bedroom and picked up the gun, cocked minutes before; walked back. The knife in the air, poised savagely, dropped instantly.

They stared at one another; this ugliest moment of the man and the woman, no truth to their titles. He vomited, again, to her pleasure, for it caused great pleasure. She said, Hello again, Prick, I'm going to kill you.

He blanched nearly down to his penis, the last hold out. She watched him serenely for it was simple, was it not? holding the gun. It was long ago that the enormity had passed over them, leaving only these brief, illuminating bits of strife and flirtation with dominance, with death, and the room was not, had never been, hers; it was the taut skin of the world he entered for plunder; she said, dreamily, I've been waiting for you all my life, Prick.

The gun fires! A monument in foam. A spray of blood, reaching, rushing, becoming the last gush of scarlet, from his chest. Like a samurai. A movie.

No.

It didn't happen. She hadn't fired the gun at all. An awkward pause, in deference to what, awkwardly, had not happened. He continued to blanch to his penis, she continued to point the gun at him; neither, in their respective capacities, firing.

A draw.

His breath suddenly expired. He sagged and puckered to normalcy. She said, You come back here again next year, Prick, and we'll do this right. A tentative truth: she was unable to fire the gun. Pendant, the brief, dry fibers of her failure, gently, twinged.

A draw, dammit. But he didn't know that, yet. A novel strategy: he watched her, cautiously, and reached cautiously for his pants, shook them at her as if to show—nothing hidden, lady!—began to put them on, said O.K. lady, I'll go now, continued to watch her fitfully, and then all that awkwardness zipped up and rushed for the door.

She barked, Come back here, you little fart! He rushed back, awkwardly, faced her, his hands in the air like a cowboy, properly obedient, obediently proper. She barked, again, take 'em off! His eyes grew round with terror; he took off his pants to reveal that astonishingly below, a dreadful sag . . . He eyed the floor, saw the gleaming tip of the knife, eyed his tender sag, thought, Awful business to have this awful woman make connections . . . She smiled, he saw her smile, she'd made connections. He squirmed, whispered, No! You can't! and with the tip of his shoe, he kicked the knife under the bed, safe, ah.

She smiled again. No, not that. Why the hell not? Because she could rape him that's why. R-r-r-rape! A teeter-totter going up going down, she on one side up, up, he on the other down, down, oh the spontaneity.

No.

He'd been flaccid since she pulled out the gun. She felt, again, those gently active fibers of discontent, for it was outrageous it was unsatisfactory it was to be deeply peeved, all for this unkillable, unrapeable idiot standing naked in her bedroom.

A draw, worsening. Perhaps: a way to live with one another? Cold war? Status quo?

The last strategy: he offered it thinking, still, of the knife beneath the bed. You know, lady, he said, you can call the police.

She hissed, the police! My dumping ass I'll call the police! He blanched again, said nothing, and thought of the knife. But the egg was laid. A solution: tall, firm, and aberrant like a tree from which the darkening fruit hung; lightly she plucked.

She grabbed his pants from the floor and shook out the contents of his pockets. She stared at this fallen, minor bundle: a sheaf of money, over $300, two pairs of earrings, a watch, a bracelet, a necklace. A thief's bounty, fit for a lady. She threw his pants out the window and left his bounty on the floor.

A draw? Not likely, she thought. The final score: he would leave, naked, with his pendant glory pointing the way; she would keep his pocket. The goods, divided. She yelled, Now get out of here, you silly ass! Obediently he left; led, indeed, by that finger of his fate.

SCHRÖDINGER'S CAT

ERWIN SCHRÖDINGER, the great theoretical physicist, owned a tabby cat named Young Werther who inspired his famous paradox on the dissonance between the world we perceive and the behavior of particles smaller than the atom. His paradox imagined a radioactive atom's nucleus, which has a 50% probability of decaying after one minute. It was to be measured by a Geiger counter attached to a hammer overlying a cyanide capsule. If the nucleus decayed, as registered by the Geiger counter, the hammer would fall and break the capsule, releasing the cyanide. This apparatus was to be placed in a sealed box with a cat. After one minute, the probability of the nucleus' decay and the cat's resulting death is 50 percent. The device, however, would be switched off automatically. Is the cat alive or dead? asked Schrödinger. It is neither, he answered, because the overlapping waves of both the decayed and intact nucleus (as defined by his equation) correspond with the waves of matter that compose the cat. The two clusters of waves are present and interfering with each other.

In addition to inspiring a brilliant example in theoretical physics, the cat was very playful and had long, delicate whiskers that came together in a wispy yet imposing beard, which often made Schrödinger think of a tiny Tibetan sage. In fact, Young Werther was the only creature Schrödinger could imagine in the hypothetical cat's terrible state of suspended animation, neither alive nor dead, awaiting the experimenter's shiny nose as the latter finally opens the box and peers in to see the only truth he cares about. Any other being would feel neither alive nor dead, but nothing. Young Werther, Schrödinger secretly believed, would feel something transcendent.

Schrödinger's face was a mass of contradictions: he had a strong masculine jaw and the tentative, pliant lips of Renaissance painting. His hair fell over his temples in creative scraggles, yet his eyes had a touch of dullness. Only the strangely rapid motion of his blank eyes hiding behind their thick glasses and dry, falling hair suggested that he was secretive. In fact, Schrödinger had many eccentric thoughts of which he told no one. Among them was the fact that he had a peculiar love both for Young Werther and for the "unreality" he had so precisely defined, a shadowy state poised between many worlds, uncertain of which it may enter.

Life was full of bitter conflict for Schrödinger. He knew that his wife and daughters deeply resented his arrogance and domineering behavior toward them. He was an Austrian father: the fact that they did not adore his dominance and fame and live invisibly in its shadow was unforgivable. These were the terms of life his father had given him with an equally autocratic will; they were as inviolable to Schrödinger as one of his equations.

A mother's dissatisfaction passes as seamlessly as dark, moving water to her daughters, who become swollen with the power and passionate release their parents are contending for. Schrödinger often thought he had been most completely betrayed by his wife. In the last year, she was often absent in the evening without explanation. The two wars he had avoided as a physics professor in Zurich echoed, to him, a world overrun by abused, violent patriarchs, all trying to seize fame, love, and the earth at once. Schrödinger, who thought that divorce was immoral, tried to lose himself in his work and was generally successful. His colleagues often joked about his absentmindedness, which was his way of concentrating on the little that was tolerable to him.

Schrödinger foresaw much of the future development of quantum physics and often described, in his lectures, the shape of the universe that would one day be revealed by mathematics integrating the four cosmic forces—electromagnetism, gravity, and the strong and weak nuclear forces. This cosmos had ten dimensions in an endless coil of space and time which was warped in various ways. Space and time had properties similar to matter: they could be stretched, compressed, curved, or twisted. They could also undergo phase changes like boiling or freezing. Defects in the continuum of space and time were therefore legion. The universe was composed, moreover, of an infinite variety of individual versions, each generated whenever a decision or observation was made. This implication followed from the operation of probability at the subatomic level: had Schrödinger's experiment with Young Werther ever been completed, for example, two new versions of the universe would spring into being, one in which the cat was dead and another in which it lived.

One day, Schrödinger spent an afternoon in his study, putting together a series of boxes for his students which could function as topological models of the warping of space and time. At the end of the afternoon, a dozen oddly shaped mounds lay on a table in his study. He stared at the boxes, then out the window at the dark, bleak winter landscape of Zurich, and suddenly felt violently angry. "It's all kinks, bugs, and magic," he thought. "It doesn't make sense." As vicious as the tensions of Europe and his family were, the universe was stranger by far.

He remembered how disruptive his family had been at the dinner table the previous evening. His wife was gone, and he ate with his son and two daughters. He had been unusually sensitive, he thought, in adapting his descriptions of his work to his son's intellectual level. His son was also rapidly becoming absentminded, and Schrödinger wanted to break through it. His daughters, to whom he never addressed these monologues, stared away from him with eyes that were huge, vindictive black pools. With round, pale faces and fingers all the more clawlike in their diminutive whiteness, the girls made him think of dreadful puppets being manipulated by something that wanted to obliterate him.

A tiny, girlish hand took one piece of white bread after another and squeezed it methodically down to a small pod of dough, finally pressing it onto the windowpane where it hung. Slowly, the whole loaf disappeared and then dangled on the window like a row of pale slugs. Schrödinger's other daughter had taken two of her hair bows and clipped them over her ears to shut out sound. She crossed her eyes and slowly rubbed one lump of butter after another carefully into her palms, knees, and chin. Schrödinger could not help observing that his daughters had inherited his own devotion to methodical, rigorous activity. From time to time, the two little girls engaged in a strange chanting, a sort of "Rrrewuu," which made Schrödinger think of witches opening ancient buried doors.

Schrödinger knew that his daughters did these things to annoy him and he never indicated that he even noticed them. At the end of the dinner, however, both girls began hacking and retching, which forced Schrödinger and his son to bolt into the next room. The girls were also bulimic, and one of their favorite pastimes was vomiting on their brother's foot. The boy uttered a feminine, high-pitched wail which particularly gratified them. In the last year, they had begun leaving little mounds of vomit outside Schrödinger's study so that he unavoidably stepped in them. During the Christmas holidays, the mounds were triangularly sculpted to look like Christmas trees. In two instances Schrödinger had, at the lectern, drawn a chart out of his briefcase to show his students the interactions between the four cosmic forces, and had come up with a display covered with vomit. Each time he made a lame joke about the Big Bang and hurriedly put it away.

Schrödinger's thoughts were interrupted by a piercing shriek. He opened his study door and saw his son cowering behind the stairway. One of his daughters had vomited over the banister on the second story and hit the boy directly on the head. Schrödinger remembered that he had seen this sight several times now; the girls were perfecting their aim. The sight of those hugely dreadful black eyes rolling away down the hall of the second story, their unknown puppeteer dancing madly on Schrödinger's grave, made him slam his door shut in terror. Where on earth was his wife? It was all, he thought, disgusting, and his son would have to fight his own battles.

Inside his study, he felt better. It must be that adrenaline rush. Out of the corner of his eye, he saw Young Werther jump into one of the boxes. Then his eyes fell to the floor, and a strange exhausted giddiness came over him. Perhaps he would wander now . . . He heard a voice, resonant and echoing, that seemed to be an amalgamation of all voices and tones; it was soothing, seductive, hostile, welcoming, ironic. It said only, "Come in," yet its implications filled the room. Schrödinger looked up and saw that the boxes were enormous. The room had expanded, and the floor looked like an endless game course, which made him laugh with relief. The laughter echoed and seemed to branch into many timbres of sound, returning from a long distance in multitudes. Young Werther, Schrödinger's favorite, was in one of the boxes. Schrödinger took off his tie. He would dangle it before the cat inside the box.

He entered the first box, which was the size of a misshapen cottage. The sight inside made him drop his tie and stare. Young Werther was nearly Schrödinger's size, sitting upright on a small black cushion. A saffron-colored robe covered much of his body, which looked almost human but for very fine fur and a hint of tabby stripes. His ears were barely pointed, and his whiskers had become an even longer and more formidable beard. His eyes were glowing dark slits which made him seem less catlike than Oriental. Young Werther had a profoundly serious bearing, which impressed Schrödinger, yet there also seemed to be a bit of malice in him. Schrödinger immediately guessed that he had fallen into one of the cosmic discontinuities about which he had so often lectured.

"What on earth is this?" asked Schrödinger.

"Welcome to nonexistence," said the cat. "It's quite a place." Slowly he raised a rather delicate, flesh-colored paw which had a tattoo across its palm. It said, "Version B72C47E." Of course, thought Schrödinger, it was a low-probability version, as was equally true, for that matter, of the version he had left. The sense of warping was very subtle, Schrödinger thought; he wouldn't even be able to distinguish it had he not just come from another version of the universe which was warped differently. Time and space, together, were moving much more slowly and had eerie gaps, which gave the scene an undulating rhythm.

"How can this be?" asked Schrödinger. "We were in my study a moment ago."

"Probability, my dear Erwin," said the cat. Young Werther grinned in a vast, toothy grimace and added: "By the way, there are many different kinds of moments here." Schrödinger instantly saw what he meant. Space warped very densely in places; there was now a heavy bridge across the cat's nose and cheeks. Yet its vacuums were numerous, irregular, and fluctuating, together forming a strangely beautiful latticelike design which continually changed before Schrödinger's eyes. He laughed at the thought of this wonderful paradox of a world in which substance itself and its unfolding in time was a matter of lovely pieces billowing in a nonexistent wind. The cat smiled again, and Schrödinger was lost in his mystic eyes—slitted, brilliantly reflective, yet full of hate that undulated in the geometry of their own green irises.

The cat changed before his eyes into a woman. In this version of the universe he, or rather she, seemed to be a rather starchy businesswoman in a tweed suit, her legs crossed carefully, still eyeing Schrödinger coldly. Her cat origin was, again, very faint: only a hint of a mustache could be seen on her upper lip, and her fingernails were a bit too long, ending in elegant but clawlike points, which were painted bright purple. The catwoman's legs were long and quite beautiful, Schrödinger thought. He was startled to come upon a new tattoo, "Version 167D490," which glided down one of her calves in seductive pink lettering. Even the stuffy business suit could not disguise the catwoman's voluptuous shape. The hint of cat origin in her face also gave it an intensely feminine, Oriental look which made her all the more exotic and exciting. She had unusually large, full lips which might have been forced out by feline teeth. And she made a very slight hissing sound which he found maddeningly erotic.

Schrödinger had never done anything unthinkable before. The hallmark of his life up to that moment was that all things, no matter how strange, were thinkable. Now he did something that was the reverse: he lurched toward the catwoman and began to make love to her. All his years of frustration with the female gender seemed to reel away from him like a colossal pink ribbon. He nearly lost consciousness of everything but his pleasure. There was some resistance in the catwoman, he thought, but it incited him all the more. At one point, a fantasy about a soldier raping a peasant woman lingered in his thoughts, but ultimately everything but his need was obliterated.

In the hours that followed, Schrödinger found that the cat was utterly shameless and came in one seductive female version after another, which he generally discovered when a new tattoo appeared in some other region of her private parts. She was all types, all women. Suddenly her ears would be curvingly pointed and her arms covered with delicate but unmistakable fur. Heavy jewelry hung from them. Then she would seem to be wholly an exotic human female, with the sole telltale sign a faint, curled layer of fur running down her spine, which Schrödinger could not resist grabbing. The sense of warping was clearer and clearer to him as time passed. Passion was the densest, most claustrophobic space and the most frenetic pace of time. He may have been making love for weeks, he thought, the gorgeous hiss consuming his life, until he at last lay still on the bed, his energy and frustration purely spent. The catwoman now held him in her arms. He saw silver rings on soft, graceful paws. This version of the cat was a young Lolita and had none of the ample flesh that had been irresistible to him earlier. She had a small bow of a mouth with a mysterious smile.

"It has taken me weeks to realize how horrifying this is," said Schrödinger. "Werther, I have no idea how to apologize."

"The perils of unreality," said the cat. "And it was you, after all, who said I wasn't real, that I was waiting for you to give me the gift of life or death."

"Surely you don't blame me for that. It was an illustration for students."

"Why should I?" said the cat. "Responsibility has so many shapes here, and injustice so many more. I have, for example, been several versions of a prostitute. I haven't enjoyed you, Erwin, yet here we have been for weeks."

Schrödinger was suddenly more exhausted than he had been when he entered the box. "I am nothing but a physicist and mathematician," he said. "How could I have intended to hurt or offend you? I only wanted to give my discoveries to the world. What can be wrong with that? Knowledge gives what little healing and protection there is in the world. As the philosopher said, nature follows number."

"Man follows metaphor," returned the cat. "Even your physics and mathematics may only be systems of metaphors."

"But *these* worlds, these versions! They are so much more complex than anything I ever projected."

"Am I so much?" said the cat. "You're the one who said I could be something so simple as a nonexistent cat, awaiting extinction in a box. But that brings unreality out of the box as well, and nothing has ever been as complex as unreality. Why haven't you been more interested in what is real?"

"What-is-real," repeated Schrödinger. "But that's what is so horrifying about my position here. You change. You show probability—now you are everything here. But I don't. I'm the same man."

"Of course, you exist! You exist and your mind is hopelessly bound to time and space. And here you are, existing in my world—the mathematics and physics that don't exist. Can you deny the fact that your concepts don't make sense to you?"

"No," said Schrödinger. "This world, these ideas, you—don't make sense. My study makes sense. Even our two world wars make sense. So what are you to me?"

"Your loves," said the cat. "All of them. The bloodless abstractions and metaphors you adore. One of them is bleeding all over you, Erwin."

Schrödinger suddenly found himself back in his study, alone. He looked around in astonishment: could he possibly have returned to his own version of the universe? Waves of unspeakable relief turned him into a nerveless lump on his sofa. But there was no more reason to have returned than to have left. So, was this still another version? Surely there were many in which he and the cat had never come in contact. The decision to keep the cat was simple enough—perhaps fifty-fifty in probability, he thought.

Schrödinger looked out the window and saw what was unquestionably a war in progress. Snaky islands of gray smoke roiled around a fierce white egg of sunlight; fiery bursts and pieces of debris fell from the sky in a desultory rain. Many of the buildings were in blackened rubble, and explosions continually rocked the house, giving it a strange, jerking rhythm, as though a huge, invisible machine were digging a pit in the earth. Why not? thought Schrödinger. A universe in which Switzerland had not remained neutral was also relatively probable.

The door to Schrödinger's study burst open and in came the frantic, bulky shape of the equally great theoretical physicist, Werner Heisenberg, originator of the uncertainty principle. From Heisenberg's freckled, bald head to the tragic wrinkles quivering below his chin, Schrödinger saw a battleground of rage and despair. Horrors marched bumpily across his face like a children's parade. "That cat of yours has been down in Gottingen," Heisenberg finally said. By this, Schrödinger knew that he meant the Institute for Theoretical Physics in Gottingen, Germany. "He's way ahead of us. Way ahead.

He's shown us all the equations for what would have been my uncertainty principle and Born's statistical work on waves. Niels Bohr called from Copenhagen—same business. The ideas in his manuscript denying objective reality have already been published by that cat. I don't have to tell you morale is very low in Gottingen, Erwin." Heisenberg, who wore overcoats that were much too large and ungainly, was an agonized, slumping rectangle on Schrödinger's couch. He raised a trembling, desiccated hand to his forehead, and seemed to be looking down from a peak in Hell. Explosions shook the house a half-dozen times before he could continue. At one point, a grenade came crashing through the window and rested in front of Heisenberg, who seemed to be unaware of it. Schrödinger leaped up and threw it out again, yelling all the while, but Heisenberg was oblivious. "I don't know how we can go on," Heisenberg said. "Can't you do anything to that cat? Didn't you once have a notion about using cyanide on him? We need you, Erwin. We're counting on you, man."

Schrödinger had some of his first real feelings of empathy for theoretical physicists. "My God . . ." was all he could say. Suddenly, he noticed that one of his daughters had wandered in through the open doorway. She carefully pulled both of Heisenberg's socks out, vomited into each, then vanished like a pale and horrid imp. A beseechingly pained expression came over Heisenberg's face; a rough laugh erupted from him. Schrödinger whispered, "Oh my God Almighty."

Then Heisenberg clicked back to his obsession like a rewound clock. "Yesterday, he had completed all the mathematics showing the interrelations between the four cosmic forces . . . ." Heisenberg's words trailed off. He suddenly had a vacant look on his face as though everything in the world had vanished. His lips moved oddly, and he muttered inaudible phrases. "Now, I don't know . . ." he said. "I'm not sure . . . but I've heard some things. I think he's been to Geneva, too. CERN, the linear accelerator. Went straight to the Gargamelle bubble chamber. He's found a host of new subatomic particles. Gave them the equations to produce them in the chamber—mesons, fermions, leptons, bosons, sleptons, photinos—my God! Do something, Erwin, and soon! He's *your cat*!" Heisenberg stumbled to his feet and walked straight into the wall. "Oh . . . ." he said, as though a great discovery had just entered his mind. Then he fumbled along through the house and stood in the doorway. Schrödinger watched him, tears of pity in his eyes. Heisenberg saw a bomb explode overhead and said, "Oh . . . ." again, as though a seminal thought had come to him. Finally, he stepped forward and landed on a mine. Schrödinger looked away as Heisenberg became many pieces of himself. "There goes uncertainty," he whispered.

A pile of letters lay on Schrödinger's bureau, and he began sorting through them. The world was now full of disappointed physicists, he shortly discovered. Poor Wolfgang Pauli—one particularly dejected letter was from him. The cat had predicted the existence of neutrinos before he could. And poor Fermi—the cat had published the equations describing the weak nuclear force first. The horror went on and on: Yukawa was no longer the discoverer of the strong nuclear force, Glashow not the discoverer of the charmed quark, Dirac not the predictor of antimatter. The cat had done it all first, and physicists everywhere were crying for cat blood. As Schrödinger continued reading the letters, he marveled that such various and original forms of murder were suggested. This was indeed a version of the universe no one could ever have imagined, for the cat was obviously the greatest theoretical physicist in the world. Schrödinger sat helplessly on his sofa, listening to the winter wind of Zurich shrieking like an ancient child and the clamor of war. Nothing seemed so unpalatable to him now as his work. The house continued to shake from sporadic explosions. He silently prayed that his species would exterminate itself as quickly as possible.

Suddenly the front door opened and the cat glided in. Schrödinger was astonished to see that in this version, he looked exactly like a cat. There he was as he had always been—all fours, tabby stripes, a tail, even a blue collar and tag. As Young Werther began to eat from a bowl of cat food in the kitchen, Schrödinger felt enraged that a creature so obviously a cat, eating its inferior dish, should have outpublished the whole worldwide community of physicists. The most unpleasant version of the universe yet, he thought. What on earth would the cat do next? And what a necessary shrinking of life time and space accomplished, he thought. To accept probability was to accept everything, anything. He knew that he was far too parsimonious for that. He couldn't stand to feel, to purely feel, his life as something like fire or light, creating and destroying itself in each instant, nothing at last but its own plenitude. A single form of time and space was the dimension of his very self. This was what it meant to be a man and not an infinitely probable being.

Young Werther walked into the study and then jumped onto the chair before Schrödinger's desk. Slowly, he arranged his tiny torso so that he was comfortably seated on his tail while his paws touched the desk top. Then he placed several pads of paper and a pen before himself and began writing equations. Schrödinger was too despondent to move or speak. As the evening passed, the cat's concentration was unbroken. He expanded the boundaries of physics further and further with no apparent thought of either himself or Schrödinger. A perfectly dedicated, blameless cat on top of it all, Schrödinger thought. What did I do to deserve this?

When Schrödinger next looked up, it was morning. He must have fallen asleep on the sofa. Bright light was shining through his windows, and the war exploded with still greater profusions of rubble, smoke, and noise. Young Werther was gone. Three paper pads were missing, which the cat must have taken to demonstrate his equations, Schrödinger thought. Who would he torment with his discoveries today? Then another great, harried physicist exploded into Schrödinger's study, brittle wrath cracking up his immense, ox-like body. It was Max Born, also from Gottingen. "That cat of yours, Schrödinger. The bitch!" was all he could manage to say. He fell into a chair, his arms flung out as though he were an enormous, chaotic piece of steak being crucified.

"What has he discovered now?" asked Schrödinger.

"No discoveries. *Worse*!" yelled Born. "Now he's gone into estrus. For hours, he's been down in the laboratory at the Institute turning tricks. Erwin, what have you done to us? It was quite enough to receive the whole of modern physics from him. But this! Do something before we've all gone crazy." Born rushed into the hallway and tripped over a small, young version of one of Schrödinger's daughters. He struggled frantically, enmeshed in her tiny legs; then the child fixed him with her vindictive stare and vomited into his outstretched hand. Born howled, jumped to his feet, and disappeared behind a violently slamming door.

Schrödinger closed his door, returned to his sofa, and stared idly out the window at the war, which was being fought as intensely as in the last half-dozen versions of the universe. Passivity was becoming quite natural to him. What could he possibly do in a collection of universes like these? His options were despair, murder, warfare, bizarre sexuality, or suicide. No wonder he couldn't get up from the sofa. Then he heard the front door open and was instantly riddled with goosebumps. What on earth could he expect from the cat now? A male homosexual cat in estrus who has been seducing physicists. A powerful, booted stride resounded in the hall. In this version, the cat was clearly humansized, heavy, and muscular. Schrödinger hid his face in his hands and waited, covered from head to foot with a convulsive cold sweat. Slowly the door to his study opened and a rather massive, dark figure entered.

As the cat moved into the light, Schrödinger saw that he wasn't as heavyset as he had feared. He looked like a pale young man with very slightly pointed ears and a bushy mustache that flared out to the sides. There was a curious striped shadowplay running over his skin and an insolent look on his face that Schrödinger believed to characterize all homosexuals. The cat sat in a chair opposite Schrödinger and smiled with a distinctly feline smugness.

"Werther, this is all I can stand," said Schrödinger. "I don't know if I'll survive any more versions of the universe."

After a long silence the cat said, "It must be terrible for you. But isn't it curious what is worst of all? Your response to the war is minuscule compared with your anxiety about your career and fame. The ultimate threat to your dominance is the sense that your life has many versions. It's more democracy and more feeling than you can bear. After proving that a single objective version of time and space is an illusion, it's no wonder you run right back to it."

"I have not been speaking for myself alone. Your grand ideas haven't stopped you from tormenting many physicists. I am also concerned about them."

"True enough, the whole bunch of you are more worried about your careers than about world war—or anything else beyond yourselves, for that matter."

"How can you blame me for so much?" asked Schrödinger. "How can a cat be so vindictive?"

"Nonexistence seems to be more revealing than existence. And it was you who articulated nonexistence as your proud creation. Now here we sit, in the midst of two world wars."

"How can you possibly be blaming me for war?" asked Schrödinger.

"I am blaming the way you make sense of things."

"But how can making sense cause violence?"

"Making sense is equal to what lies outside the window," said the cat. "As your metaphor, I am your means of making sense. Your metaphor has just a hint of something as elusive yet whole as a child dreaming of music. You lost it as you moved further and further away from your origin; it has all the shapes and tones of emotion you no longer hear or feel. You find a momentary, worldless beauty which seems to return your self to you. In telling you this, I am also the only moral force in your world. Your metaphor is your child. Treat is as carefully as you would a child, for it is your first blind step away from the truth."

"I see myself," said Schrödinger, "as a relatively simple man who does complicated work, and whose major failing is something so plebeian as absentmindedness. How does this fit into your great scheme?"

"Ah, your wandering mind!" said the cat. "I am terrified of the implications of your wandering mind. The end will come ultimately not in violence at all, but from that vast inability you have to feel the consequences of your thoughts."

"What should I have done?" asked Schrödinger. "What should I have given the world? I gave my equations, my family, and I am very sorry to say that I gave you, my metaphor."

"Another annoying aspect of the truth is that it is always in front of you," said the cat. "Just look into one of my eyes."

Schrödinger looked into the cat's eye and indeed saw a world both exquisite and strange. The cat's iris was a glowing, green-layered geometry arranged about its own vanishing point, the pupil. Schrödinger smiled. "The more I look at this, the more it reminds me of what I wanted to say in my physics lectures. The complete universe is a perfectly symmetrical topology disappearing at its own center. Here it is in miniature, right in front of me . . . Perhaps I should have given this to the world. I would just have held it up to all of them—everyone whose life I could not touch—my wife, Gottingen, my children . . . ."

"I'm not giving up one of my eyes for a bunch of physicists and bulimic little girls," said the cat.

Schrödinger laughed for the first time since entering the cat's universe. "You'll have to pardon me. I keep trying to use you literally as an illustration. I believe that's what started this business."

"Poets try to do this sort of thing without pulling out anyone's eye," said the cat.

"Oh poets . . . ."said Schrödinger. His voice trailed off. His mind was wandering.

In many versions of the universe, Schrödinger is still peering rapturously into the cat's eye. He meets with a small frustration, however. The cat's eye is not stationary, of course, so in its reflected surface he must see a grossly distorted image of his own face. This seems to be the price of the cat's vision. There Schrödinger is now, over and over again—elongated forehead, nose, and chin—an homunculus rushing from one direction, then another, almost (but not quite) obscuring the slitted vanishing point into which the face will one day truly disappear, and never be reflected again.

The cat, on the other hand, is a subtler, more lucid thing, shimmering with his own light grace. He leaps and glides throughout all versions of the universe, never so long in one place as to achieve substance, something more like all of light and motion, always suggesting something else, always haunting, the truest and most elusive ghost, never quite repeating; when all is said and done, darting into his own vanishing point and then arising from it again.

CARMEN'S ANSWER

I CAN'T LISTEN TO Bizet's "Carmen" without twisted thoughts. And, there I was, painting an exterior window trim on the second story of my house, sipping wine and listening to a compact disc performance so exquisitely real that I had the whole sweaty bunch with me. I both admire and hate Carmen: she's the woman I have the questions for. Specifically, why are we never able to control passionate love? Why do we always fall in the kettle again, impervious to learning, maturity, sensible embarrassment and simple, sheer fatigue? An argument with my lover the night before lent urgency to this question. Carmen should know the answer. For the last century and a half, she has not been the creation of men but great divas, all of whom comment on one another's renderings in their own performances. Carmen is therefore the image of uncontrollable passion as it exists in the imaginations of many women. A collection of images is all we realistically know about any experience. Somewhere in the portrayal of Carmen lies an answer to my question.

After three days without love-making, I begin to sicken. Over the next few months, I come down with all the symptoms of a kind of lust ague: aches in my joints, pulsating headaches, shortness of breath, even a dripping nose. Of course, I do whatever is necessary to regain my health with the greatest possible haste. Limerence is the latest word for it, a terrible neologism that makes me think of copulation in day-glo colors. Some combination of my inebriation, self-righteousness, and a vague mystical tingling gave me a vivid sense that Carmen had answered. At that moment I tumbled, in passionate union with the mezzo-soprano, off the ladder—landing two stories below with a broken leg. Now, forget Carmen (the bitch). There is only pain.

My shrieking could apparently be heard for a long city block. I held nothing back, uttered hideous sounds, and immediately attracted a flash flood of onlookers—alternately bald and fuzzy heads; the smell of sweaty Nikes and a carton of pizza; a bearded creature with enormous lips, peering and hunched in pure fatherly regard; a woman blowing her nose; a dog's consoling tongue in my ear; and Carmen still crying for "la liberté." Then a tidy, gleaming ambulance whisked up to save me. A swift, rectangular structure wielded me up and down, then deposited me into the ambulance's maw. Well-fed, it began to shriek, and I joined in for a raggedy, dying yelp.

Whatever they injected into my hip for pain unveiled a fabulous montage of all the women I had ever loved. Yet somehow, it had begun before I fell. Love had no beginning or end, only pitfalls and bumps, I explained to the nurse who asked how I was feeling. Couldn't she sense its livid heart in the wail uttered by the ambulance?

"A talky one," said the nurse to the driver. "I think we've got Demerol, shock and alcohol mixed up here." With this, she gave up any attempt to have a conversation with me. A rueful smile twisted her middle-aged face into the lumps and skewered edges left behind by all the exaltations and despairs she must have swallowed.

"Hell of a headache coming," said the driver. "Won't remember a thing." I vanished into a collective knowledge of extremities and their inherent deceptiveness. What could a fall, a broken leg, and an ambulance have to do with love? And how could I explain when love was perhaps the emotion swallowed least and remembered best?

I closed my eyes and began a silent dialogue with myself on the nature of love. How awesome, after all, was the power of memory; at any moment, what a brimming over of other people we are. My lovers peeked out from the blank wall my memory had been. Joining one another through similarities in eyes, lips, hands and hair, they drew together into a web. When all they could be lay in their relationship to me, what dangerous, treacherous creatures they were. The force and intricacy of memory is dazzling and paranoid in equal measure. My lover's ironic smile of the previous evening, doubting everything I said to her, hung ominously over the web like the smile of a Cheshire Cat.

There was my first love, now a smudge with two teeth missing in a photo, an eight-year-old brownie scout in my mother's troop of raging little girls who could, at childish whim, bounce like gumballs. Today, I am a blonde Amazon of a woman, with hands and feet so large they can make me think I am the subject of someone else's surrealist painting. I bolt through life with my near-bionic limbs, a Swedish testament to the physical expanse possible to womanhood. This body is sufficient to be loved. Then, at the periphery of my first love, I was two or three years old, roughly half the size of a brownie scout, which meant I had to work carefully.

I ignored her until an hour or so into the scout meeting: a tangled mass of tiny, brown-swathed bodies rocking back and forth in cardboard boxes; rubbery limbs jumping over all that lay still in the world; a soprano roar moving up and down the scales of sound, distinguishing nothing but what was purely wonderful and what was not; enclosed within a livingroom and den; my mother startled to be at the center of this mass, a mother, somehow justifying to herself that she controlled its protean brain and limbs and even improved it. My mother knew, unlike those who believed the brownies to be a survival of rural values, that these children were an early inkling of the chaos which can be squeezed into a single uniform, and eventually into the multifarious category of womanhood.

I saw the moment when my brownie was still and made my move. Rushing to the girl, I grabbed her around the waist, buried my face into her navel, and hung on like a little bulldog. The pandemonium of helpful children grew to a crescendo as one girl after another tried and failed to pull me off. I held on with the radiance of my love, all the star-crossed lovers implicit within one lumpishly determined little form, my blond curls in union with her abdomen, separated only by the sash of patches she had earned for being normal.

I may have gotten away with this spectacle a half dozen times. Then, in dreadful humiliation, my mother gave up her brownie troop to some other mother whose household could better maintain middle-class conventions. I remember the first week that passed bereft of brownie scouts. My mother looked deeply into my cherubic face and feared all that lay behind its apparent innocence.

That is the narrative of the events. But the resonance of the memory—how it stirred to a fullness and vanished—that was something else. I remember little response to the separation at the time it occurred but, through some elusive physical association—a girl's pale hands; a bent, running figure in the distance; the lightness of childish noise; even a particular late afternoon light in dusty air—then there was a shower of pain that removed me from the present entirely. The force of such memories rarely diminishes with time; rather, it maintains the power to shut one into a flickering, breathless world of pain in which all other physical details are suppressed. The sound of an ambulance siren in the distance has always disturbed me since it aurally expresses such an eyeless world of pain for the person enclosed within it. Nonetheless here I was, smiling with my eyes closed in an ambulance, shot up with a delightful pain-killer that had made me giddy with memory. The more I considered it, what a chimerical thing my memory seemed to be, for which was my first love—the narrative or the resonance? And, which ambulance was the real one—the present or the imagined?

Something in that little girl's face, perhaps a pout around the mouth and chin, reminded me of a woman I loved when I was thirty. In many respects, she was a child—of thirty-five—with a resentful mouth, suspicious eyes (which are darker than any others), and long, glorious wheat-colored hair. In her face was the angry girl who had rebelled against her domineering father. She told me that religion was the core of her life, a claim which always arouses my suspicion that a conflicted, half-violent, emotionally desiccated relic stands before me. Our first date was in keeping with my fears—a trip to an unheated church on a winter night; specifically, a brackish medieval pile with a wooden roof which leaked dark, oblong drops of rain suffused with the smell of earth and moss, all cataclysmically mixed with an odor of wet animal fur.

In a freezing pew, she whispered inaudibly intense things about her love of asceticism, then grabbed my shoulder and pressed her hip against mine. I was suddenly distracted by the thought that there might be a frozen cat or two in the adjoining pews. Nothing but shadows entered and left the building after absorbing their diet of bare, frigid penance. A dark pew was a perfect place for a stray cat to rest. Who of all these worshipers would even notice if the whole church were filled with frozen cats, their rigid, crumpled forms suggesting the most abject penitence?

On our second date, she elicited a promise from me that we would not make love until she felt that spiritually she could make this "negotiation with God." The most devastating aspect of her faith was the belief that God caused illness or death in those he regarded as evil and that Christian Science "healings" were a means of survival. My promise of complete abstinence aroused her terribly, and we made love within 15 minutes.

How could I have loved this woman? The layers of memory had still not revealed the critical truth—what had made her lovely to me. Perhaps it was this: As adults we bewildered one another, but as children we played. I remember a magnificent kite she made to fly over Walden Pond on the first day of Spring. It portrayed a nun barely escaping the jaws of an alligator. She had worked with amazing care to make the nun's gown, and the alligator's jaws, billow in the wind so that the nun jumped as the alligator chomped.

She also painted skeletons as spiritual essences reclining in deserts, and once we had the only conversation I've ever engaged in on the subject of my skeleton—specifically, whether I might will it to her if I died first and equally, whether she would keep it in a closet or her livingroom. Eventually, the only way I could change the subject was to say that I knew perfectly well she would stand naked before my skeleton and place its bony hands upon her breasts. With a wistful smile, she answered that indeed she would. I told her I could not allow my skeleton to be used for this purpose, and that was the end.

Yes, the end. As we made love more frequently, the conflict between sexuality and religion became greater for her, and she began to perceive me through an even more bizarre sequence of images. She wanted to cover an entire wall of her house with a painting of me as the archangel Lucifer, rising from Hell in a feathered cape. She had even begun saving bird feathers from assorted neighboring lawns and walks in the woods to make the painting more realistic. As the first sketches went down on the canvas, I felt a wrenching combination of anger, pity, and the remnants of love. Her ex-lover also hovered on the wall as an enormous mass of charcoal lines, incomplete because she had fled for undoubtedly the same reasons I would. I had seen two other huge canvas chrysalises in her basement: All of her lovers had left before she could finish the painting. Who, after all, could tolerate being thought of as an archangel rising from Hell?

We had arrived at the hospital. I could not open my eyes and sensed only hands touching my body as I was moved from the stretcher. I tried moving my fingers to prove I had conscious control of them and could not. A compulsion was dragging these thoughts and memories from me and strangely, I was not disturbed. It seemed both necessary and inevitable. Hands touching my body became my final impression of this brief experience: I was being touched by a person I could not see and who could not see me. This impression illustrated the great difference between the love a child and a woman feel. The child's love is pure impulse, imageless. For a woman, there is a continual interruption of mental imagery tied perilously to memory, so very profuse and distorted in this particular woman, eventually turning me into a body that was touched but otherwise existed in layers and layers of images fused with fear, at last rising up from nowhere as a monster she called Lucifer.

Images. Then I caught myself. I was resting so comfortably with my image of her, as tranquil as one can be in a hospital. And, if I intended to lie still and speculate, then I needed to know what I thought an image was. Image: a partial view of a phenomenon which attempts to suggest the whole, not recognized as a metaphor but as an actual belief. Its complexity can range from a single visual image to a narrative of many impressions. Images are both true and false: true in that they can evoke a response or experience credibly and intensely, false in that they are never truly the whole they portray. Hence, I have at least two contradictory images of my brownie (the narrative and the resonance) as well as two contradictory images of the ambulance. Images cannot, therefore, be defined, though they can be portrayed (my present activity). They are nonetheless our basic means of perceiving wholes, without which we would have little extended memory, emotion, thought. Love and its undoing are both tied to images. As truth, images have tremendous power and may be the most deeply felt content of memory. Love begins exclusively with the feeling aroused by an image of the lover and may never again be as intensely or profoundly felt as it is in this state. As untruth, images are equally profound. In the insufficiency of the image, its inability to portray the whole, is the root of misunderstanding and suffering.

Then what is memory? A matrix of images continually revised by the evaluation of what is both true and false in it. As I experience memory, I therefore see a world of images whose truth and untruth are always changing, often beautifully so.

This is the territory I am now exploring. This is what is happening to me.

And for the moment, the most difficult image of all: my lover's ironic smile last evening. "How strange you still are to me, after years," she said. "You have such a fascination for people; you're a voyeur or a crazy metaphysical detective. You always want to put all the pieces together, and you won't stop brooding until you do. But when you live with someone, day to day, you're always imagining that a cataclysm will occur. Are all writers like this? Why are you so at ease with anything that's complicated and so doubting of anything simple, like our life and our happiness together? Why is that?" Years ago, she said almost the same thing: "You give a much better description of an imaginary person's feelings and motives than you do when you try to explain why you are suddenly so afraid—in our home, on a Sunday, as though it were your last day on earth." With the most tender irrelevancy, I am always struck by how lovely she seems when she says these things: the softness of her body and her hair (I must hold her at these moments) and the brown specks in her eyes which make them a grave, compelling green.

The story I was telling myself began to have plateaus, falls that did not end and, finally, daylight. It began again with a headache, a hospital bed, a toothless woman snoring vigorously through lips that flapped like the opening to a tent, and my toes thrust up like little pink soldiers out of a white cast. The sight of my broken leg was strangely satisfying: the wrong had surely been righted and the mess cleaned up. My toes had never looked so clean and competent. Since I had nothing to do but stare at them, I could continue the story; which pleased me until I recalled, in astonishment, that it had induced paralysis the night before, a paralysis I was content to accept. As I sensed the other narratives beginning to form, it came to me that the story was filled with images which had never been assimilated: they were the failures, too ridiculous for memory, things that had long ago created boundaries and passed across them. They were hiding in a more vulnerable part of my memory, and I was reaching it through illness, a drugged ambulance ride and a drugged sleep. For that reason, the story had to go on. And, in the light of day, with their broken legs, the lovers and loves hobbled on, and on.

For a very long time, I loved a woman who, had she lived in a pioneer wagon train, would have found some way to both crack the whip and pull with the oxen. Her drive and her need to control were so extraordinary that she regularly pulled the world up by the roots, slapped it into shape, and told it what it surely intended to be. It was partly this arrogance, raised fully to myth and almost to poetry, that I loved in her. She was the furthest remove from my religious love, who moved through a heaven of preconceived images, then was constantly shocked by the disappearance of Lucifer. No, my greater love made images herself, then demanded that they be alive and true. There is a certain violence in both of these styles.

There are as many reasons to imagine me as a pleasant incompetent as to fear I am Lucifer. One point of view implies that I am a toy; the other, a shadow. The reasons may even be the same, for how are the results of incompetence and divine punishment to be distinguished? She had plenty of reasons to decide that I was not to be taken seriously, and she was not above reciting them: I had tripped over the television while walking in my sleep 13 times; I had no interest in money or competition; I fell asleep in public places; did not sweat; dreamed of other lovers; lost my driver's license, birth certificate, and other I.D. cards with great frequency; had spells of agoraphobia and once had to be carried down a Mexican pyramid by a guard who was half my size; spent many afternoons and evenings as a student trying to find the books I had lost in the morning; was pierced in the knee by my own metal boomerang; had periods of melancholy so intense that I resented the existence of light. We both knew very well I had once been so depressed that I tried to drive to a mental hospital but couldn't tolerate the neon glare of a gas station and ran out of gas, depositing myself on a freeway shoulder at

4:30 A.M. What do these acts signify? They said, according to my lover, watch this one carefully or she will put her boot through your television, fall off your roof and mangle your lawn-mower, toss a cigarette butt and melt your word-processor, leave indelible blood in your swimming pool. She is a lovable jinx.

Her image of me largely shaped the ambivalent love I felt for her, and the narrative of our life together is therefore predictable. Do I have any memories of her uncolored by a bit of resentment? I see her on a day when we were driving across the country with our two pet dogs. The dogs were both middle-aged males, a husky and a samoyed, and they spent their lives despising one another. Though they were only two in number, they were obsessed by the fact that the husky was dominant over the samoyed. This enraged the samoyed as much as anything on earth and I, whenever I saw them together, knew that he thought of little else.

I do not know what it is like to abhor a moist snout covered with caramel-colored fur, be followed by flecked eyes that see nothing but inferiority, and perhaps be pursued in dreams by two dark pointed ears. What I do know is that while my lover drove, the dogs exchanged places with one another continually in the car and when this trading of territory occurred, the samoyed attacked the husky and was defeated. The two dogs therefore breathed, paced liked wolves, were attacked and defeated over and over again, which caused my lover momentarily to hate them as well. Their ritual was altogether too repetitive and too familiar.

When we left the car to eat, she always put the dogs outside on chains, one attached to the front bumper and one to the rear. On this particular afternoon, however, she was utterly disgusted with them and went immediately into a roadside restaurant, leaving them alone inside the hot car. They fought all the while we were eating and when we returned, the samoyed had just been killed in the back seat of the car. The signs were incontrovertible: his pinkish skin was blue, his eyes were open and immobilized, and the husky was still keeping the strangle-hold that had cut off the samoyed's air supply.

My lover grabbed his dead body and crushed it to her breast, crying uncontrollably. It hardly mattered that she had caused it. He was dead, and she loved him. But her drive and her need to control were at least as great as her love. The woman in this story was a very successful college professor, to become a dean within two years and a college president in four. She could outpublish and outmaneuver any competitive snout that came close, and her political instincts were as acute as any animal's. She was, in short, not going to let this little piece of white fluff disappear without storming the empyrean and grappling with death.

Paramedics! she thought. Artificial respiration! She hoisted his limp body out of the car and rushed it to a grassy spot, then grabbed his wilted snout and blew and blew into his mouth as vigorously as the proverbial west wind. His wet nose was held in her grasp so no air could escape, and she blew through the enormous layers of his mouth and tongue all the way into his chest. His lungs filled with life-giving air—again, again! Then, while continuing this maneuver, she grasped his tiny, forlorn paws and pushed, then pulled them—in, out, in, out! She blew, wept, raged, and blew. And lo, there was a flicker of an eyelid. He twitched, he breathed. The samoyed was raised from the dead! In another 15 minutes of voluminous blowing, he tried to rise but could only wriggle in the grass. The husky was utterly fascinated and nosed the samoyed's little white snout almost fondly. He received the faintest bite in return.

The end of the story is that the woman loses a lover but gains a samoyed. No, I can't remember her without resentment, and perhaps all memories are mentally rewritten in their last instant. Perhaps my own memory and imagination mislead me as much as those of my religious love.

Yet the image of gentle incompetence is hardly the most oppressive I have ever absorbed. My earlier life was the time for that claustrophobic, compulsory embrace called family, school, home town. Only a child's long, barren wait for years to pass can earn the right to leave it. The images imposed by these deceptively small groups are among the most powerful and rigid of our acceptable daily tyrannies. We begin our lives in domestic fascism, regardless of the political philosophies of our governments, and some of our best Hitlers are the adolescents produced by it.

The casualties are the angriest and subtlest of us. I remember the radiant, oval face of a black girl of 19 or 20 in a chartreuse dress which swirled around her luminously perfect body. Its bright color and irregular pattern suggested huge tropical leaves and feathers, all of a startling beauty against her ebony skin. Her oval face was a perfectly shaped painter's harmony of line and faintly glowed, as if it were carved from black marble. Within this delicate symmetry, her large dark eyes held an exotic weight. She could have walked out of a rain forest.

The dress was a lover's secret between us. A fiercely competitive male queue followed her around for hours at a party we both attended, all fluffing their plumage, but none knew until the end of the evening that she had worn the dress to please me. The queue had no idea how vulnerable its arrogance had made it. As we left the party, I imagined many pairs of shocked eyes peering at us from a huge pile of multi-colored feathers which lay on the floor behind us.

We were students then at a west coast college during the '60s. Where did I first meet her? We were lying on the floor of a cabin in the woods with a dozen other students heaped chaotically on top of us, all grinning at one another like tickled infants; this was briefly an American custom during the '60s. We saw nothing but patches of a wood ceiling through wreaths of blue jeans; boots; gym shoes; khaki and gabardine shirts; army peacoats; thick, worn vests and belts; ubiquitous androgyny the color of swamp; all exhaling the hot, uncompromised, grassy breath of our generation.

Known as "group sensitivity," this phenomenon occurred over the 2-3 days of a weekend. It began with a collection of students talking about intimacy and sincerity as though they were the equivalent of football players tackling each other; this was called "confrontation." It was derived from an intuitively apparent universe of rage and confusion. The event quickly proceeded to group physical exercises—holding bodies, lifting them, stroking them, even unclothing them.

The order of events was this: The most hysterical members first identified themselves in endless, tortured monologues and received these physical ministrations like a sacrament. The group then pummeled each member with hateful observations, all true by the criterion of intrinsic hatefulness, followed by a silent stroking, lifting, and heaping of bodies; hence all were confronted with hate and love in a perfectly regular but incomprehensible rhythm. We therefore generated the most instantaneous, superficial images of ourselves, then followed these revelations by pantomimed responses which implied a range of emotion, yet were nonetheless based on equally artificial images. The human heap, which came at the end of each hating and loving session, was intended to show the group's intimacy, unity, and joy in these activities. If asked for our tender thoughts, we would all have replied that this was the most revealing experience to be had, and we intended to do it the very next weekend. Altogether, it was the creation of a generation rife with image-making, all cut loose from the domestic bindery at once.

At the bottom of the last heap, no one but I could see her hand as it slipped into mine. Had the group, which envisioned itself the furthest evolution of all-acceptance and honesty, known that two lesbians were holding hands at its bottom, we might all have had a few cuts and welts as the whole heap tried to rise and move away at once.

By taking my hand, she had given me a sign whose meaning was clear, since it could not be a response to anything but the campus' image of me. My notoriety for joyous, heraldic, unabashed lesbianism was almost legendary. All response to me was based on this single fact of my existence. To this inescapable social world, I lived solely to engender lust or fear. In this light, any girl who put her hand in mine could intend but one result, seduction and infamy. Deeply touched by her courage and trust, I reached over and kissed her fingertips.

Shortly after that weekend, we spent an evening together, walking around the city, as absorbed in the drama and strangeness of our life stories as if we had washed up on an uninhabited island together. The night sky had rolled over the billowing orange clouds of sunset and enveloped us in delirious, dark purple; the distant lights were a sparkling necklace lying around the hills as we laughed, talked, and wordlessly knew that we wanted nothing more at that moment than to be lovers.

Her life as a story was full of sudden, radical change. Her parents were both university professors in the south. She had grown up in a white middle class milieu and found other blacks more difficult to talk to than whites. The black civil rights movement was the most exciting thing in her life, yet it presented her with conflict. Few blacks involved in it had come from a sheltered and comfortable a life as she. To her, the net drawing blacks together was their language—jive—which she found very demanding and felt she "spoke" poorly.

Shortly, we were so enthralled by our closeness that we invented fabulous deviant pasts and described them to one another in jive. We sold drugs, prostituted ourselves, ate mushrooms and hallucinated, bombed cities, ravished dormitories, murdered rapists, etc. in jive. Within a half-hour, we were completely disoriented and madly in love.

And, if jive was a foreign language, she spoke it magnificently, an African queen of a charismatic, reeling world. She was far too verbal and clever to do a poor rendition of it, despite her anxiety, and as I listened to her, I silently worshiped both the woman who expressed herself in this astonishing way and the woman who wanted to bring together the dissonant elements of her life.

At the moments when our energy ebbed, she told me many other stories from her past. I was confused by one of her erotic fantasies—finding a white girl unconscious in the grass and making love to her—but nothing could detract from my feeling for her uniqueness, presence, beauty, and the half-wonderful contradictions of her life.

When we returned to my house, I invited her to smoke a joint with me, an obligatory polite gesture in the '60s. As the familiar curiosities came over us—enhanced colors and textures, a bit of obliqueness in the heart of life and its attendant paranoia—she suddenly imagined a church of young blacks shouting at her, full of vindictiveness that she should want to make love with a woman and a white one at that. The joint had subtly increased the range of my perception while suppressing my ability to speak. I wanted to reassure and convince her that she could overpower these images springing up from the past as I had done; images having great power but embodying the values of other people, not coming from her actual self. There were no words to say this. There was only a quiescent, shimmering world-texture that could be touched but not elucidated. As my silence continued, she suddenly walked out of the livingroom and climbed the stairs. I had no idea what she thought or wanted. She was unknown, a dark figure receding.

I don't know how much time passed then. Suddenly, I used the sound of my voice to break the paralysis. "If this house must have one new madwoman," I said, "then it will have another, as well." Whereupon, I rolled four joints, poured two tumblers of wretched, cheap wine, and fell upon my fatal feast. My intention was essentially to blow my brains out—without the gun. I had an overwhelming desire to make myself crazed, find her again, and rave along with her. Shortly, my teeth were as empurpled as a movie vampire's from the foul chemicals in the wine, and I was coughing over a small marijuana bonfire.

Reality #2: The world was formerly split in pieces, but is no longer. The pieces have simply disappeared. I can see the contents of the livingroom, but both I and the house are nowhere. I walk into the back yard and look at the dark, pour another tumbler of wine, swallow, belch, stumble, and fall into the grass. The dark is everything. I might be falling through it, but I can feel the soft, bristly earth cupping me.

Reality #3: She leans over me, kissing every part of me, cosmically at ease. How could she ever refrain from this, she seems to be saying. She slips her clothing off almost angrily. This is the way she was meant to be. I am all a-fumble with buttons, zippers, shoe strings. Her body is breath-taking under the light. There are bluish waves sweeping over the perfection of her shoulders, breasts, running down her inner thighs. She has the widest, richest smile I can imagine. Her body is an ideally proportioned, timeless carving of God. I will never be able to think of God without seeing this ancient woman who is the most beautiful embodiment. Then I understand: through the most circuitous path, I have become the image she is seeking—the white girl lying in the grass. I take her face in my hands and say, "How did you know how much I wanted a black girl to find me in the grass?" We both laugh and begin our hungry devouring of one another.

It is no small pleasure to laugh with a goddess. And, to make love with one makes a silently raving mystic of me.

Images of the '60s: spirit, love, peace, liberation, expansion of consciousness. They are difficult enough to portray if individuals are creating them, but groups—

this is almost another level of reality. I see now that I have been on this level for some time and my story's images are multiplying, all the while the conflict between what is true and false in them grows greater and memory spongier, less reliable, and strangely enough, more moving. Yes, images are the most deeply felt content of memory. They influence us in spite of their incompleteness because their lyrical power makes them unassailable. Perhaps my generation was a collection of haunted aesthetes, drifting from one beautiful image to another, vulnerable to nothing but a new generation which lacked imagination.

I remember a girl of 18 or 19 who had so many images crossing her life as to be, virtually, a myth. I met her in the campus coffee shop during the late '60s, and I was roughly her age. Archetypally, she was completely naked, talking heatedly to a group of students. There were so many young men crowded around her that I couldn't get close enough to hear.

She was the classic Botticelli of the '60s who emerged from the features of innumerable tall, blue-eyed blondes wearing their hair very long for the first time. From her gestures, I could see that she was aggressively challenging the people around her. The image of nudity, to her, meant authenticity and almost spirit. Everyone was therefore exhorted toward an inspired shedding of clothes. No more should the campus be ruled by denim, khaki, gabardine, leather. I could see that no one was convinced as such; at the same time, a nude espousal of belief was utterly compelling. A version of the image passed from her to the crowd. It said, if she takes off her clothes to say it, by god she means it.

I later talked to other students about her and composed her story, assembling the images that made up a private mythology, just as I am doing now with my own life. The crazy metaphysical detective, as my lover would say, is up to it again. I don't know the point at which I began to love her. When I closed my eyes, I saw her thickly tangled, tawny hair and the softest, round dispersal of light where her body curved—lips, breasts, knees—as though she had powdered herself. The image returned again and again. I was too young to struggle against obsessions; my own life still coursed images like a fountain.

The Living Theater, another staple of the '60s, had performed on campus the week before I met her. She and her friends had seen it and were very moved. I saw the performance as well. The cast was completely naked and also regarded nudity as a symbol of enlightenment. They turned down the lights, banged drums, leaped from the stage to the audience, and rushed around like hairless baboons, from time to time grabbing a viewer and dressing him or her down with words, slaps, and (often) spittle. The oldest of the group—a violently emaciated man with a face as severe as the apocalypse—jumped onto the laps of a man and woman and cried, "I am love!" I instantly recognized that this, like my group sensitivity, was another version of "confrontation." The image imposed upon the audience was that it must be timid, unloving, uninspired, shallow, insincere, and inferior because it was clothed and shocked.

In the '60s, people were as apt to feel guilty and inferior as to feel aggressive and superior; these two groups sought one another. The Living Theater was able to find many appropriately guilty pairings for its aggressive acts and often seemed clothed in light for its noise and spittle. At other times, an actor came upon a pair of bottomlessly dark, dubious eyes that stared through him and his flimsy soul and was unmoved. At these times, reality seemed to have a certain weight, something these monkeys of spontaneity couldn't begin to portray. Then, we noticed other aspects of the performance— the fact that all the actors and actresses were terribly skinny, the level of noise, the fact that we really wanted to mill around with a beer in hand.

Behind these images and gestures of attack, I sensed great rigidity and artifice. The girl I loved was predisposed in a different direction, however. She was the daughter of the American ambassador to various Moslem countries and had lived her whole life in the Middle East, up to the time she left for college. A tall blonde, she stuck out from the native population, and if she did anything beyond what women in purdah did, the Moslem men could do frightening, unpredictable things to her. The line beyond which she couldn't pass was always unclear, because the men also had some experience with Americans and regarded themselves as reasonable and partly Westernized. When their violent, fanatical side emerged, they also rationalized and believed she had done all the more to deserve it.

Teheran was the most unpredictable city, in this sense. She lived there during her teens, when her father was the ambassador to Iran, and unintentionally endangered herself several times. One afternoon, the weather was warm and balmy after long rains, and she put on shorts and bicycled to school. The image of a girl with this degree of pure bodily freedom was one of those dark stones that dropped straight into the men's thoughts and stirred poisonous waters. One of the deepest, most inclusive images in their minds was that a deity which held total, incomprehensible power over life and fate, with whom no mediation was possible. The rigidity of the image, paradoxically, gave it the power to effect a greater range of emotions and hence colored their sense of justice, freedom, ritual, gender, even sexuality and spontaneity. The sight of such a spontaneous act from an American girl, implying nothing but independent, biological life, much like the nudity she would later advocate, drew Allah to the world's edge and left her just as nakedly exposed.

The men who saw her resolved their conflicts by quickening their steps and then running after her, finally throwing rocks. One man, very close, whipped her back with a metal chain. She was as frightened as anyone might have been. As images seethed in the minds of the men, terror made a pure blank of her own.

While the ground was level, the bike was a great advantage and she sailed along. Eventually, the streets were more cluttered and broken up, and she could no longer move as fast. She had no idea where she was going. The streets became darker, poorer, more filled with stench and refuse. At last she threw down the bike and ran. More and more men added themselves to the chase, both young and old, and she knew she couldn't stay ahead much longer. Eventually, she came to a cluster of half-ruined buildings with a small meat market watched by an old woman in purdah. Some freshly butchered animal carcasses lay on a crate turned to its side. She slid into the crate and quickly rearranged the meat over its top until she could not be seen.

The men ran past and on through the labyrinth of the city and its poverty. She could see out of the crate through a tiny slit, which showed more buildings in ruin as well as a large shapeless stone that could have been either a statue or part of a building at one time. The smell of bloody death penetrated her to the bone and the soul, and her tears mixed with the butchered flesh covering her. Suddenly, she saw the old woman, and her heart stopped. She stared at the dark stone, trying not to think that someone now knew where she was and conceivably had the power of life and death over her. She let the stone fill her mind entirely.

As moments passed, she realized that the woman would do nothing to expose her. She sold several cuts of meat during the afternoon while keeping the crate's surface completely covered. One of the men kicked the meat savagely as he passed, which left the girl's shoulder immobilized in pain. Under the carcasses, she felt the world as a single, hideous thing like the stone, and her life shrank to a shell. Blood slowly entered her mouth and stung her eyes. The most horrible thing in the world, she sensed, is a single thing. Just one object, like the stone, completely alone and held by a void.

She waited there until the men stopped running, fell back, and began to return home. At a certain point, they began to laugh and smoke. Something of a celebration started up as the sky grew dark. She could hear singing and briefly saw a few moves of a line dance. The men touched one another's face and shoulders and hugged. When it was completely dark and quiet, she came out from under the carcasses. The old woman, who was still sitting in the crumbling hulk, rose and limped toward the girl. She removed the scarf of purdah and handed it to her. The girl looked at her arms and legs under the moonlight and saw that they were almost completely covered with blood, which had now hardened and looked black. She placed the scarf over her face and head. The woman pressed the girl's blackened arm and returned to the building ruins. The girl watched her for a moment—the being who had held the power of life and death—white-haired, frail, and tiny in the pale light. Then, she began to walk home, avoiding men wherever she could. The city was so poorly lit that her blackened body was hardly visible. She walked for many hours before she even knew where she was. Very late in the evening, she arrived home, unlocked the gate, and threw the scarf aside. When her mother saw her, she screamed. Again and again, she explained that the dark, clotted blood was not hers, that she had no injuries, she was not wounded. She told the story in a monotone and did not cry.

Hours later as she lay on the bed, very clean and quiet, she knew that some part of herself stood totally apart, rigid, and dead, like the stone. The image of a crude, half-formed statue in bright sunlight came to her mind at odd moments for many years. It was the horribly single thing left in the void, the power not of life and death but death over life. Silently, she understood that she now shared this truth with the men who had chased her: the stone was Allah.

When she was 18, she arrived at college in the States, rid of Moslem men and their culture for the first time, and decided to shed every physical fear and inhibition that her past had taught her. This was shortly before I met her. She instantly became a kind of cross between a cave woman and a naked social worker. She consciously passed from one radical experiment with her life to another, disinhibiting and bodily improving herself and as many others as possible. From nudity, she progressed to the deflowering of young male students reputed to be virgins, during the full moon on the dormitory lawn as a good example to others.

She constantly weaved in and out of my life as a pure superlative: the demonstrator with the largest sign, the one who slapped the loudest policeman, companion of the largest number of young men, bearer of the most ungodly clothing when clothed. At one point, she was adamant that no one should wear shoes. Throughout the winter, her feet were bare as she trekked about the campus. I occasionally thought I had passed into a time warp when she strode by me, covered with snowflakes on a winter night, the penance of Valley Forge on her face. At the campus Christmas dance, a formal occasion, I watched for her to see whether she would consider wearing high heels. She arrived in fish-net with hose on her feet, the slightest condescension. At the center of all these images incorporating the body was the day her body, doing no more than living, had almost been murdered by Moslem men. The vitally alive, spontaneous body was the image of dissent, rebellion, and salvation to her. The '60s was a groundswell of images, and those she generated found their place among others and persisted. It astonishes me that she was ultimately little different from other students; such is the leveling power of images.

I found her one day covered in blankets at the library, talking intently to a friend, her feet resting on a chair. She was so engrossed in conversation that I thought she wouldn't notice me as I studied the soles of her feet. They were covered by enormously thick, wedgey layers of calluses with great ridges and gashes running over them. As I looked more carefully, they seemed to have familiar regularities in callus thicknesses and clefts—almost, it suddenly struck me, a tiny city occupied by cliff-dwellers. Thoughtlessly, I touched one of her feet as I imagined the towers and transportation lines of the cliff-dwelling Indians who could live in such a structure. I had almost located their water supply when I became conscious that her conversation had stopped, and she was closely watching me closely watch her feet. She put her hand on my shoulder, gave me a deadly, blue-eyed stare, and said, "You have weak, pale feet, don't you?" Her voice was suddenly as gravelly as a chain-smoking truck driver's. "Think about it: why do you *really* wear shoes?" With that, she left. It was a provocative question, the like of which I have never again encountered.

To her receding, blanketed body I said in a disappointingly small voice, "I'm probably in love with you." There was a hint of startled flinch as she heard me.

A day later, she came up to my dormitory room. Against the gray, barren walls, a woman with such animal force was a shock. For a moment, it seemed as though a great, blonde lioness had devoured my lovely Botticelli and now waited, unmoving, to polish me off. She was wearing a dress made of green yarn, half-finished, and she took it off as soon as my eyes met hers. Her hair had just been washed and ran down her shoulders and back in blonde rivulets. It was the first time I had ever seen it combed. Again, I saw the faint, soft light about her body as it curved, and I wanted to touch her with an unbearable passion, but did not.

She wasn't bothered in the least by my silence. I was another novelty to her, a way she had not yet liberated her body. Her body as an image was very powerful; it had obliterated Allah. But whether she fully existed beyond it was terribly unknown. She could have no idea how much I had learned about her and the painstaking portrait I made from it. And, she would probably have little grasp of the hot-headed, story-telling creature I was, full of my own quirks, images, bumps, and darkness.

There are things I deeply desire and yet deny myself. Not many, thank the goddess.

I simply bolted from the room. My regret was unspeakable.

My track winding through love, history, and culture was cut short by a tiny ancient man with silver hair who suddenly appeared and bent over me, touching my leg and cast, apparently a doctor. I was just going to ask him whether he was real or another creature from my imagination when he said, "You have a malleolus fracture of the lower part of the tibia and fibula as well as a portion of the ankle." That settled it—my broken leg was real. "We have it pinned and casted," he continued, "and we've been checking for circulatory problems. I think we'll be releasing you sometime in the late afternoon."

I talked to him briefly and discovered the uncomfortable fact that all of my thoughts about love, image-making, and memory had occurred at the expense of the present. My presence in the hospital for the last 18 hours (of which I had no recollection) was a wonderful candidate for the most ridiculous experience of my life. If they didn't serve me a dose of pain-killer every four hours, I would yell and keep the ward awake. When I did get my shot, I would tell anyone nearby the ongoing saga of my love life, for which I had imagined myself the sole audience. My lover had also been to visit me twice and, along with the hospital staff, become so concerned over the bizarre content of my stories as to think I might have fallen on my head. When no head injuries were found by CAT scans and EEGs, I earned a slightly cleaner bill of health and was set up for an early release, provided I did nothing to warrant placement on the psych ward, which was by no means certain. How a doctor can tell someone these things without laughing is beyond me. He oozed authoritarian calm and seemed to be of another species. I would have much preferred to have a venerably wrinkled old elephant with a waggling trunk come and tell me how outrageous I had been.

The cause, as I noticed in the ambulance, was obviously the pain-killer, which released my hoard of stories from me. I could not really feel vulnerable or taken advantage of since there would perhaps be no pocketful of stories at all if I had not unconsciously used another sort of pain-killer: Images are also a means of avoiding the truth. The stories had come pouring out of that fact as much as anything else. I decided to quietly accept the blunt, growing ache in my ankle, slowly radiating throughout my leg, which demonstrated that the pain-killer was wearing off.

Since I had a few more hours in the hospital, my story continued with a question: which images contain many others? What is the whole that the particles keep trying to mimic? I can only say that I once saw something like this, but now accord it no more belief than any other image that has moved me. Life does not really fail to give us visions. We often have them, but only as images, which are always called into question and reshaped by the present. There is a vision in my private mythology, a night when I saw a mysterious red light behind a city skyline and thought it said more about love than any other impression or experience. Now, I can marvel at the simplicity of my perception that night. I was as young and porous as I have ever been or will be. I nearly believed in magic. The red light was magical.

The night fell shortly after I broke up with a lover and returned to graduate school. Two days earlier, we made a last trip to a small Mexican border town which was remarkably like the village I lived in as a very young child. I deeply regretted the uprooting of my life, and the town seemed to reflect a stabler, simpler existence. For hours on end, we walked through the streets, mesmerized by endless groves of flowers, jets of red, purple, and orange bowing in a grace of heat; rows of tiny houses painted and decorated with great care, as though intimacy depended on it; people clustered in the town square or on street corners, seeming to believe (as we did not) that a city was theirs; an open window revealing a funeral bed inside a home, as though death were not something apart from these people; even the dust blowing over the beautiful whorled wood floors of the cantinas, both a substance and a rhythm moving in an ancient, far greater dimension of time than ours; at last the stately, symphonic arrival of the stars, as clear and profuse as in a desert. We did not see the poverty, labor and frustration of the people, though they were there to be seen. We saw the image which was solely their love growing around them; it was as true and as false as any other image I have created and believed in. We both knew that at the end of the day, we would separate and have only a relationship in memory to the town and to one another. That made its beauty intense to the point of pain.

After I returned to graduate school, I couldn't sleep for two nights. I spent the time walking through the dark streets, holding a vigil I could neither articulate nor stop, hoping that I might be able to exhaust myself. For long periods, I sat beneath the late summer trees, watching the massive, uncontrolled growth of the branches and leaves. The dark paradoxically gave them greater breadth and wildness, an effluence of energy that rendered them unrecognizable. They virtually seemed to be creatures, both plant and reptile, impossibly alive. It was as though our world only existed in daylight. At night, the foliage beat us back and became fertile and monstrous, drawing the earth to a beginning in which we would have been destroyed.

On the third sleepless night, I drove to a lesbian bar in the city center. I had often come there in the last year and enjoyed both the company and the atmosphere. In wooden panes throughout the interior were stained glass windows showing male and female historical figures in gaudily colorful scenes. The period was recognizable in most of them: medieval, renaissance, Victorian, etc. The scenes tended to be melodramatic—wealth, passion, violence. The rest of the interior was as spare as a monastery, so the whole effect usually amused me and I toasted many of the scenes. I drank two glasses of red wine, lost in my thoughts, and then went outside to an alleyway where I smoked a joint. I expected relaxation, fatigue, something which would send me home to sleep, but that is not what happened.

When I returned to the bar, the tables and bartops were glossily reflecting the intense colors of the stained glass. Robes, swords, beards, stones, trees, animals leaned over them in elongated bursts of color, color which swayed and bled wherever the women were sitting. As often as I had been to the bar, I had never seen this violent human kaleidoscope before. Faces leaning over tables had huge casts of orange, red, blue in chaotic, turning shapes. Hands in the light had striations of green, brown, purple as they moved. The explosions of color, light, and gliding shape seemed to be another world that had lost all coherence and reached from the glass to the women, all the while they talked, laughed, gestured and knew nothing of the root of their world.

Stunned, I left. It was outside, when I looked at the city skyline, alone with a cool wind blowing, that I saw the red light that was love. Almost a red powder, a delicate physical substance lay beneath the darkness of the buildings, bridges, water, even the sky. If I had returned to the bar at that moment, I knew I would also have seen some evidence of the light beneath its tumultuous surface. The leaves and even the dust blowing in the air followed a hidden rhythm that emptied into the city's love. The reflections of light on buildings, the fire and oozing darkness of glass, the shifting edges and boundaries moved with fabulous shapes and textures, all of which were transient forms of the red light. The whole world was infused with love, centered in love, moving, speaking of love. This was our answer to the daylight beauty of the Mexican town, which seemed to exist centuries before. We had inundated our whole beings with the splendor of images. In its plethora was its lack, endless cities of lovers who would move from one dark body to another, who would never be satisfied, who would imagine, throb with the images of love for the rest of their lives.

And my life. I quickly found my way through the crowd inside the bar, past many faces of women, to a woman whose stare arrested me. She was small, very dark with full, red lips. I don't remember her name; I don't remember what we said to one another. That is not part of the story the city tells of its lovers. I remember every inch of our skin. A red candle she had lit burned lower and lower; its light was the last splash of color I saw when I was exhausted. Then I could sleep.

Meaning does not exist apart from its material; love is shaped by image-making and memory. At the center of this unfolding is a fountain of images—consciousness. As a reflection of the world, what a shifting, tumultuous thing it is, a darkness filled with dazzling half-truths. As subjective experience, how moving and filled with meaning these half-truths are. Images are words we say to those we love. The unique attribute of love is that it draws images together, binds them with a force of its own, makes them tell their tale. I suddenly remembered my fantasy that Carmen had answered my question. What could that answer be, after all, but the images I have made of love, a story focused again and again through the lens of memory, coalescing just for a moment, the way I had spent the last 20 hours?

The most profound love reveals the only face we ever see, imageless. I now understood why my lover had said that simple happiness frightens me more than complexity. Our relationship was almost devoid of images. We had time and intimacy to wear them down, soften their edges, until even the boundaries between us often seemed ephemeral. If we were not just as we are, I would lose everything and return to my jungle of images.

I phoned my lover; there was nothing more important. And, in an hour or so, in brutally bright sunlight, I walked—or rather, hobbled with a crutch—out of the hospital. I hadn't a single bizarre story to tell anyone. It took my lover a day to notice a change. She finally asked, "You've been suspiciously quiet and serene since the accident. If you're not careful, you'll begin enjoying your life. What's up?"

"The crazy metaphysical detective has gone on to other pursuits," I said. "The crime has been solved."

"Hmm. But the mystery deepens."

To that, I had no answer.

THE STATISTICIAN

YOU MUST KNOW ME: I'm the man who proved that the percentage of rodent hair and excrement in the average candy bar is .00152. If you've never heard that one, you've undoubtedly come across another of my little firecrackers, that the average annual income of a San Francisco prostitute is $74,189, and her age, 23.4; that 302.9 acres of forest are expended for one average Sunday issue of a major metropolitan newspaper; that 272,154 children are employed annually in pornography; that the national tonnage of cats and dogs killed each year by the A.S.P.C.A. is 39.8. Statistics should be called the study of the morbid and bizarre.

I run, in short, one of those number-crunchers that supplies all your newspapers, TV schedules, best sellers, business seminars and science symposia, not to mention those hard-working gamblers of our body politic who use numbers to control everything from your svelte nuclear warheads to the grubby contents of your wallet. Don't think so? Try bumbling through life without a dozen kinds of insurance; try spending your childhood years without the bell curve shaping you more boldly than your body could ever attempt; try receiving any form of medical care—toothpaste to open heart surgery—without someone appraising the odds of your pleasure and payment for the outcome.

Only saints and the brain-damaged escape being polled and sampled throughout every moment of life—by your friendly politician, scientist, salesperson. It's the only issue upon which they all agree. They must count your favorite innocuous activities, your pocket money, your blood, your genes, your ballot. You are a flesh container of this primordial soup of numbers that feeds all industry, science, premeditated violence—clearly our most important activities. We live as specks within interlocking webs of measurement that make us all mad relatives, number-obsessed kinsmen who eternally count one another and never utter a word. Remember the dream in which you are standing naked in a well-dressed crowd, unable to find your clothes or control your anxiety? Numbers have stripped us in just this way, while we mumble them over and over and imagine we control the world.

Do I sound bitter, miserable, full of hate? Not at all—it's just more number-crunching, business as usual. After all, I'm a statistician, the only one who is paid for counting. The rest of you lambs are just counted in your sleep. I run a relatively unimpressive, medium-sized business consisting of a small analytical chem lab and a minicomputer with CADD and graphics, all run by operators and programmers whose work makes them personify random numbers over any other state of living substance. Do I sound as though I hate them? Why? they do just as I ask—carry out statistical analyses for marketing studies, scientists, bureaucratic snoops of various kinds—largely means, correlations, spread sheets and verifications of statistical significance, producing, in other words, nameless, faceless, numbered exhibitionism over all other means of identification.

At times I am strangely moved by numbered quantity and feel there is a mysterious fitness to it: 17 milligrams of shattered bone clinging to the blueberry bushes beside D.B. Cooper's unopened knapsack of cash; the fractal structure of coastlines, clouds and Gregorian chants; the positive correlation between violent crime and the full moon; the quantitative perfection of fish bodies for movement in water, birds' wings for air currents. Numbers bear witness and no more, and so doing may occasionally lie in the silent, beautiful domain of angels. There is even a coarse beauty to sheer number without measure—the myriad of dead creatures humming in our auto gas tanks, the elements in our bodies that once glowed in stars that died long before the sun's birth. How can creation and destruction commingle so in quantity itself? Here the multi-colored, endlessly various world of life and death passes beneath my keyboard and ritually I acknowledge it without judgment—the godlike Observer whose glance caused time and space to erupt into being and explode a universe. Too much? Hardly; the random has always been regarded as the sign of God's presence, that which is beyond our control. And I suppose we can't forget the input of the 15th-century street gamblers, who needed a convoluted Renaissance rationale for their cheap thrills. Who can blame them? If we didn't have our means and correlations, we would be naked as cavemen, afraid to come out into that chill, unsparing light we moderns have let fall on us.

All right, I am bitter, and I do hate my co-workers. But I'm the company president, and I can do it with abandon. What is this frustrated anger that has unleashed my small, pathetic torrent of numbers and words? As I look out my window, I know it is this hatefully beautiful autumn day with its frail, blackened boughs and riotous colors hovering in air—so perfect a mingling of randomness, beauty, life and death that I can never separate them—something meant to seduce me before I even touch my keyboard. Strangely, it is less frustration than a devouring loneliness—I who produce the nothing that is, in other hands, the essence of everything. I have an inconsolable desire to see and touch one of my products. How bizarre: I actually want to talk to a mean.

Now, my Mean would be the average of various attributes of men my age, 42, with exactly the proportions, personality, interests and financial health I am so efficient at measuring. So why couldn't I just pick him out of a crowd? I know more about him than his wife does. Isn't he, in a sense, my "better half"? Isn't he "truer" to life, the inhabitant of that blank surface I am always reaching toward? Why wouldn't I, of all people, take the greatest pleasure in capturing him?

A fantasy life is particularly dangerous for a man in my profession. For all the phantasms of probability, I at least can be counted the empiricist. I am, therefore, anxiously delighted to be ducking out of my office so suddenly, then walking in a random direction on a random street. Here I am, trying to find him, all the while making certain my motions are only those of chance, for how else would I find him? We are on the saint's only pathway together.

My imaginary adventure is making me giddy. Yet why couldn't there be another world superimposed on this one? The street is a plane over which my means and correlations are gliding with secret, ambient life—as real as anything else. The route to them lies not, ultimately, in a step-by-step direction but in the larger pattern of diffusely random motion. If I accept the limitations of total randomness, I move in all directions at once. As I passed crowds of people on the street, I was pleased to think that they saw a human being as real as themselves, yet this one had left their universe entirely.

I remembered my first vivid impression as an adult—the one that signalled, beyond a doubt, the end of childhood. It was the sense of an invisible pane of glass secretly separating me from all others. Now the pane has merely hardened, become another way of life, and all that lies beyond is cast into a kaleidoscope of shifting, random shapes.

I also recalled a thought that once frightened me: the dead continue as they are. They congregate on the other side of the glass, ready to divulge their great secret, only to realize it is too disappointing for belief. Perhaps I was now hovering with the dead, the absence of life unspeakably mundane. What words, after all, could describe my adventure? "The president went out for lunch and disappeared." Or, "the president pushed an invisible button and snuffed out the world." That was truer, for I sensed my adventure had an element of hatred. Why should anyone contemplate with ease this man passing on the street, myself—the taciturn man with lifeless eyes? He lives in another world, he thinks.

Doesn't this make him an assassin of life rather than another of the pathetic, silent dead?

I never answered my question, yet I walked for hours, the streets turning blander, my mind deadly in its emptiness. Slowly, I began to discern signs that I had passed into another world. In some elliptical way, my experience began to show different patterns and dimensions; whole constellations of events that had never been significant before were now of the greatest importance. I was losing my constant "where," a great roving "eye" of perception that opened vantages, discerned processes, assigned beginnings and endings. Rather, the world was becoming the "how" of its assembly and packaging. It pressed upon me with weight, density, more like touch than sight. It bore me away where I had always stood apart. There were no processes beyond fluctuations of a serial. Totally unpredictable things, therefore, said *life, here, now*—an elevator, for example.

It was as though I had never experienced an elevator. How amazing, I thought, this is just what I was looking for, each floor a compartment numbered with lights. We stand in our little block of space, watching the floor numbers while the chain of occupants fluctuates randomly. Here for one-two was a gaunt man of fifty with flaring, gristling sideburns and jowls of resignation, meticulously lined, as though he had carved them tenderly himself; followed on three-four by a young Hispanic messenger whose clear, olive skin glistened and challenged the world, the skin of Indians and Orientals alike, patches of a race going up or down in power's own probabilities. At five-six everything changed since we reached the advertising agencies: the softest, widest-eyed girls in the world, girls who seemed to nestle when they were still; and young men in light suits carrying coffee, whose thin, ironic smiles seemed humiliation spoken in another language. When I came down, nine-eight was a chaotically stained technician, overweight and dripping, thinking of something and someone else as he smiled in his distraction, and a hard-on rose indelicately in the grimy folds of his pants. Then, at two-one again, I stepped out with a bustling queue of middle-aged secretaries—the shortest strides, the varied hues of tinted hair—I, the great leader of randomness with my followers, whose identities shifted like the senseless code of their tiny, tapping heels.

So you see, I was spending my afternoon traveling up and down in elevators, then disappearing soundlessly. I had to admit that I was having a wonderful time. I should wander away from my work and into another universe more often, I thought. Yet nothing in my new world was as truly satisfying as a subway—a work of both random drama and art.

The subway car's center most intrigued me, since it held two long rows of seats facing one another. Perhaps a half-dozen to a dozen people were constantly lined up, side-by-side, opposite their partners in exact randomness. Here was an old man with hair thickly scooped up like an ancient president and such huge, attentively sensitive ears, a bit of a donkey thrown in, altogether the picture of energetic servility sitting beside a woman, obviously poor, whose face was a mass of wrinkles and ridges sloping downward, as though she had sucked the earth and found it rotten. A languid, young man of Thai-Cambodian origin had a face that was a study in curves—the startling, sheer roundness that can be eyes, the ears high, tapering orbs like the handles of coffee cups, a low bulge over cheekbones and a nose so round and low it almost slipped away—all was dreamy, wave-like, unfulfilled. He sat beside a balding Italian man with huge, curving lips, drooping mustache and lumpily slanting eyes, somehow so seamy, meaty, sweaty he seemed to want a wall to pound his fists on. Close to him was a rumpled old woman with a huge bag of refuse, obviously her only possession—furry, glinting eyes beneath general filth—who every night must throw her old-rag's body on the ground, grin toothlessly and crawl into her bag. Beside her was a creature of ambiguous race and gender, like some young projection of the future where all contraries have been resolved, the confusion passing, even, to the jacket—denim with deerskin fringe.

Now I had quite a lumpy little Mulligan Stew concentrated into the two rows of seats, drawn together by their random appearance. Their isolation from the rest of the car immediately suggested a kind of tale or journey in action, with all seats filled by my protagonists. As some left and others arrived, I asked myself, what is my unfolding tale? The stew was presently dominated by the limp Southeast Asian, who would sink into some voluptuous shadow and resist any initiative; the seamy Italian, who would be enraged by any suggestion; the man with the president's ears, who would merely tremble with the pleasure of being told what to do; and the old bag lady, who would scoop up the journey's garbage and save it for posterity. The tale would therefore seek a presence to give it direction and inspiration, and we had only a moment before this influence arrived: a black girl of thirteen, already immense, with huge pink sunglasses and madly dripping curls, who cracked her gum as loud as creation—she would lead us all.

At some point in my long, playful monologue, an inexplicable terror began. As strange and vital as I found this little compartment of humanity, of tales and adventures begun and never finished, it was not alive at all but frozen in some eerie way—rigid, fractured, dead. I was wrong to think that I saw an inner life in these people. They did not emote, but grimaced. Their vividness was a function of the severe pose into which they were incomprehensibly locked.

The woman sitting beside me became a mass of twisted lines, then a mask rent by terror and despair. The mask's contours crumbled into a chaotic paste or clay, then hardened into an expression of insane delight. She contorted into one emotional grimace or posture after another. How had I seen this as alive, even amusing, earlier? Or was there still another imaginary world into which I had stepped?

The man with the president's ears was now convulsed into an unmoving expression of horror; he resembled a ceramic mask of a Japanese actor far more than a human being. What was happening to them? To me? I was terrified and tried to bolt out of the car, yet my legs locked for no apparent reason, and I fell into the center instead. When I touched my legs, they registered no sensation at all. I tried to bolt again, but my legs only twitched on the floor in a strangely mechanical rhythm.

As I looked up, a world of tortured grotesques surrounded me. They hovered above, each face a mask. Real feeling did not exist in this world, but had been replaced by arbitrary contortions.

I did not want to touch my own face.

At that moment, like something in shadow at my vision's edge, he came to me. He was standing in the front of the car, holding one of the overhead reaches—a man with unusually regular features and a closely cropped beard. He was totally unlike the others. There was no convulsive motion on his face at all, only an intent stare ahead. He had a strange luminosity, something tenuous, only partially revealed, as though he were coming in and out of focus. Where the crowd was frozen and contorted, he was elastic, graceful, almost brimming, as though he possessed some spiritual force. He seemed totally oblivious to the repulsive human detritus collecting about him.

I had found a Mean, my original reason for conceiving and entering this world. He was beautiful, which filled me with horror. The last thing I expected to find here was something beautiful, lit up with an inner light. Strangely enough, something in my stare filled him with horror as well. He turned and looked at me with an expression of hate, as though I were something more horrible and distorted than the crowds. I looked away, frightened, and when I next looked up, he was gone.

My legs touched something solid, and I lurched out of the car. I tried to run after him, but my legs seemed frozen into a single position. Consequently, I weaved back and forth, as though held from below by a magnet. Sliding through the subway corridors, I saw one frozen face after another, a play of grotesques.

Finally I slid up the subway stairs and into a spare, rectangular green park. A dying tree provided me with a bench, and there I waited, gasping, for the Mean. I could either pursue him or wait for him—we were that close.

I sat for an indefinite period, watching the denizens of my new world come together in spasmodic groups, then shoot away from one another as though repelled. I sensed a strange order to their movements. They weaved and slid until they "arrived." Arrival was a moment in which they composed a random assembly, after which they had no more reason to bond and broke apart. At each of these gatherings, a different emotion contorted their features and gave them a new, artificial pose, as though all they could become was a link in a random serial motivated, in turn, by nothing more than a desire to be counted.

Then it came to me: This world was identical to the one I had left, except for its lack of pretense, empathy or apology. Here we lived to count one another and for no other purpose. There were the inhabitants—most revealed and defined by the random movement of one to another and its brief pattern—an elevator, a subway. This was our version of identity, friendship, even love. Any and all emotions could be portrayed or summed up in these bizarre assemblies.

I saw a man walking a dog. Even in the dusky air, he had the fluid, shifting surface of the man I had seen earlier, the play of light and shadow so quick, he seemed effused, glowing. This almost spiritual quality seemed buoyed by its distance from the grotesques and their antics. Here was another Mean, yet how different from the previous. This man was much older and heavier, with a great, dark, brush-like beard, unkempt. He habitually looked at the ground, then back up to the scene at an angle. I could see no motive for this strange act; it was as though he didn't want to look fully at anything but rather to see a series of tightly angular distortions.

I approached him slowly and raised my hand. I didn't want to startle or repel him as I had the other Mean. If I recognized him as a Mean, he might know that I was virtually the reverse, a man. As I came closer, I saw that he was even coarser and filthier than I'd imagined. He stared with lightlessly dark, suspicious eyes. I had no idea what to say to him. Here we stood in the remnants of light on the city's tiny island of green. I could say, "I am a statistician. I made you and then I had to come after you." Or, "I made you and then there was nothing but you." This was truer.

At that moment a rough, heavy fist hit my mouth, then the man seemed to fall away. I was lying on the ground, my lips throbbing, the hot, mineral taste of blood in my mouth. No one else saw what had happened. The people continued their spasmodic associations and darted away alone, oblivious.

I sat on the dead branch again, lightly touching my lips and chin. Still, I could think of nothing but the Mean. Why had he attacked me? And above all, what did he know about this world that I, as a man, did not? My obsession impelled me as forcefully as his fist. I had to find him again, that or another Mean. I couldn't rest with it.

It was now twilight, and the park began to empty. A parade of grotesques filed past me and into the street. Brisk shoes drummed along in perfectly regular rhythm, eyes bulged and mouths gaped, elbows bumped outward in what might have been chaotic but for an awful synchronization. What a twisting, lurching, drumming throng they were, held together by nothing but pantomime, amputation, repetition. How I despised them. Now a fat man was laughing beside me in great heaves more like sobs. His gaping mouth began to bend oddly and then purse itself into a bitter line while his eyes rolled upward.

"You puppets! You horrors!" I yelled. "Are you alive or dead? Can't you tell me?" More heads rolling. And eyes. Oh, such eyes—glazed, terrified, rolling, slack, squinting, petrified. Eyes of extremity but lacking depth or light or feeling. Hands reached to touch me—fingers splayed star-like, small pointing daggers. "What are you!" I yelled again.

There were tears in my eyes, on my cheeks. I reached out to the grotesques, either to hit or touch them—I didn't know which. My face contorted into a ferocious grimace that closed my eyes and bared my teeth while tears streamed down. Rigidity was overcoming all attempt to communicate, and the sound from my throat was a whispering babble.

I heard a deeply discordant sound—irregular, shuffling footsteps in the street behind me. I turned and saw an indistinct, gray figure. The elasticity of its movement instantly identified it as a Mean, and I lurched after it, rapt. My own movements became more elastic as I approached the Mean.

It was a woman. She had that elusiveness, hidden life held apart from this ossified world. Her movement was slow, rhythmically unconscious, beautiful. I was astonished and relieved at once; I had not imagined a woman among the Means. As I followed her, I found that I could move spontaneously at a certain distance from her yet became even more contorted and rigid when I was close, suggesting another dimension to this world. I was entranced, even more compelled, than I had been with the others.

She turned toward me after the next corner, aware that she was being followed. The last dim fingers of twilight heightened the contrast between the tangled mass of her dark hair and luminously pale skin. Her eyes had force, solidity, tenacity. As I stood beside her, my limbs clenched and revolved mechanically into strange, warped angles. I struggled against the contortions but became even more distorted and monstrous; my slight inclination toward her convulsed, exaggerated itself, and at last I was a dark, predatory mass. As though we were both beneath a sudden rain, I had the most acute sense of my own skin: minute pinpricks of shock inundated me as she watched. She was seeing a man who had turned himself into a monster, a pulp of twisted reflexes hardly different from the grotesques. Her dark eyes absorbed what I had become, sharing with me the most perversely intimate moment of my life. I tried to ask, "Don't you know me?" yet my voice was nothing but horrible, whispered vowels, incomprehensible.

She walked away from me. I could do nothing but follow. Then, something even stranger began to happen. As I approached her and she turned, I no longer saw a woman at all, but many isolated vantages of one. I was close—to no more than her hands reaching out and her jewelry, faintly silver, falling against them. Or, I had a glimpse of her neck vanishing into her blouse and framed by tumbling hair. This happened again and again as I pursued her: graceful hands lighted by rings, somehow all the light and shadow on earth; hair that fell torrentially down her back and became a darkly frothy world; the line of her cheek and its secrets—this too was a world. What was she becoming? Something at once whole and fractured, beautiful and distant. When I had absorbed this, I returned to the jagged prison of my body, as repulsive as the grotesques.

This world began to grate horribly. I was constantly losing her, then regaining an image, a fragment I wanted all the more. She seemed wholly spontaneous, yet was her purpose not to allure and then frustrate, leaving me with nothing but my own monstrosity? I was struggling, grappling, yet with what? The most fragile, tentative, dream-like of materials. The strangest thought of all came to me: If I could complete one action, one effort to communicate, with my feeling and thought entirely sensed, this world would come tumbling down. This world was a chain of masks and images.

I lost her again but went on, looking everywhere for what could be no more than a sign—a hand opening, the swell of a cheek, the fullness of her hair. Then I was against her and we were touching. I watched her hungrily, exploding—and at last I knew what would free me. I hit her. I did it again and felt a rush of pleasure. My contortions were gone, and I was in control of myself: that was what I truly wanted from this world. No, it would not come tumbling down, but here was something almost as satisfying. I picked her up and slammed her against the wall. When her dead weight fell back into my arms, she was mine. Then my dark joy filled the world. Her nose and lips were bloody as she lay with me, nothing but the loveliest, darkest weight.

Night enveloped me. It was darker and somehow deeper than I had ever known it. I searched the horizon for half-light, wind, motion, but sensed only this pure and even dark. At last I welcomed its dissolution and slept.

I awoke in a strange rush of white light, alone. It was morning, but the familiar sounds of birds, insects and distant human voices were not around me. There was only a rhythmic rustling made by the grotesques as they passed. My skin was dry and hot, yet no strong impression—thirst, color, motion—came to me. Like the night before it, the day seemed curiously purified, dissipated and absolute. I scanned the horizon but found nothing but this palpable lack, the white light's blank network. I so anticipated physical sensation that the vacancy itself became a sound, high and whining, now pouring out of the sky.

My limbs were so rigid that I could barely move. It took close to an hour to prop myself on my elbows and sit up. The process of standing was even more arduous, yet I welcomed the struggle as an alternative to the sky's utter blankness. As I finally stood upright, I saw a man standing directly before me. Or rather, a Mean.

He said nothing. An amused, bitter light danced in his eyes, and he grinned broadly at my discomfort. His face and hair had a soft, fragile glow; he seemed almost androgynous, which contrasted with the exultant, sadistic smile on his face. We both understood how complete my decimation was. In this world, I was almost a paralytic, even more amputated than the grotesques.

He reached out and very lightly tapped my chest. I collapsed like a shattered vase, and the sky was filled with his lithe, young perfection, a demon lit up with angelic light. I want to say that he attacked me, but that is not quite it. As I lie on the ground, I can see everything against its background, the great blankness, and my life is clarified, brutally. Rather, what I have become completes his violence, and from this moment on, I know exactly what will happen.

It unfolds like a serial I've seen before. It has both the explosive violence and the order of this world. It was, after all, an admirably impartial, amoral system of numbers that generated the Mean—and made me need him. Now I need his violence. He hurts me in every way—his agility, his laughter, freedom, truth—everything I have surrendered to him. How can I even curse him? His acts, at their roots, are numbers—the language of nature, the language of God.

I am completely frozen with my eyes closed. Any physical function surrendered in the world of numbers is irretrievably lost. Yet this world survives, becomes greater for my paralysis. I do not need my sight for the serial composes the scene. Perhaps I see it more clearly now.

The light is pure and harsh and the day hot. The white metal of the sky shrieks. Its blankness is a godly lucidity. I feel the violent clarity, the utter simplicity, of this world like the moment of creation, the unalloyed dawn. The Mean is still standing over me, but I am more aware of what surrounds us. It is an edifice, perhaps a building. I have a sense of great antiquity, jaggedness, in its fine detail. As I follow every ridge and pore, frozen finger and declivity, I see the whole history of my life's distortion. It is all that has been erected beneath the sky and resists the brilliant white daylight. The grotesques shift before the door, but their antics no longer disturb me. I did not see, until this moment, their sacred awe. No one actually passes through the door. Rather, they contort to all that is probable, had they done so. It is a creation of meaning itself—necessary, human.

At the edge of my vision is a flower. I can no more tell you what flower it is than what it looks like. It is too simple and too complete. Even my motion through this world is flower-like, the peeling of one image from another like petals, until I come to the substratum of reality. I see myself at the start of my journey, staring at the twisted, ancient foliage dying outside my window. In its bursts of red and orange, it whispers to me of my need for violence. I am a man, utterly alien to this world. I am that handy, hollow thing, so clever at cutting the world in shares and counting them. And I end in the contradiction of numbers, the truth that severs all from its context, its nativity, until the sum is this pure, flower-like, violent world, without mercy or hope.

And its living things. Why should they treat me kindly? After all, the Mean is the ideal; I am the aberration. He is the truth—I, the artifice. I am a man, the one whose feelings are no guide, no touchstone; but only vague, soft pressures, below sense, like numberless insect wings beating in the dark.

Something stirs in the doorway. A Mean is passing through it. I am awed by the whorled, rippling surface of its body: supple, genderless, complete. Seas, forests, continents are its flesh. They are hair, skin, force, contagion. It engenders a universe and thrives, as I cannot. It is beautiful, and even beauty is my intimate as I pass over the edge. I try to hold the moment when the Mean's cool, agile fingers first circle my throat.

APOCALYPSE

LATE ONE NIGHT in the year 986, a strange object fell from the sky. It was flesh-colored with brilliant flashing lights and observed by a rather unstable monk of the Order Vicarium. The monk, who had never seen such a thing before, charged breathless through the foliage that covered the grounds of his monastery, leaves and robes mutually flapping, threw open the great oaken door and shrieked, They are destroying the world again!

His superior, asleep in a great oaken rocking chair, stirred profoundly, rolled her eyes skyward, and sighed, Again! For a time they shrieked and sighed respectively, then Mother Primora said to her sweating, gushing initiate, Grimoldo, What shall we do?

Grimoldo shrieked at the top of his voice:

> Make gestures of appeasement and reason—Publicize total unpredictability and savvy at once—Narcotize our populace to glisten with confidence—Privately send spies to the prairies—Arm all surrounding territories—Reconvert our economy to attractive and comfortable battlegrounds—Reconvert our spies to cadets—Invent more bristling technologies—at last send grinning ambassadors everywhere with death warrants or faculty positions upon their return!

He paused to let it settle as best it could.

Mother Primora only sighed, Again! The two stared at one another with the pregnant silence of an absolute. Then Grimoldo screamed, I forgot! I forgot to pick it up!

What? drawled Mother Primora, rocking to and fro gently.

That thing! was his last shriek, and Grimoldo streaked back into the black like a trained seal. Mother Primora kicked the great door shut with a fierce flutter of her skirts and thought, He is irresponsible to the point of idiocy. He has utterly failed at all but shrieking prophetic monkhood. She gritted her teeth solemnly and kicked the door again, pleased at the flowing design of her robes as they settled in place. However shall we program the condominiums of our battlegrounds, she thought, how surreptitiously council our witches and astrologers, how brandish, how bridle technology further. Ach well, and she cuddled up in the rocker again, but then we would never know about another final destruction without these unstable fools. They're the only ones who know when it's the end again. Softly, she rocked to oblivion and dreamt of flesh figs brightening hypnotically to vermilion; swelling, they rounded to baubles, swollen they fell, *pock*, and Mother Primora climaxed in her sleep.

Meanwhile, Grimoldo fled into the dark forest surrounding the monastery. Exquisitely plotted, cultivated, and terraced verbena and Spanish mosses wound their tendrils about his arms as he ran. Crocuses, hollies, and snapdragons planted by centuries of perfectly socialized monks clung to his ankles, stuffed his sandals. At absolutely regular intervals huge hot leaves and giant petals smacked him upon the ears and chin, for the forest had been designed for sensuous sauntering at large and not for hysteria. He flopped upon the murky, overcultivated earth at last, covered his eyes, and saw eons of patient workers both smiling and shaking their tools at him. What? Oh yes, the end! he thought. Night, flight, and terracing had utterly befogged his mind. "Unidentified flesh object," he tried. No. Just as well, "unidentifiable flesh objection." But they'd know what he meant. And his purpose was to find it, to hold it with trembling hands, to give it to someone else.

He jumped to his feet again and ran past the misshapen hut of Professor Woof, the Calculator. Briefly reflecting that he had no reason to be fleeing Woof, he rushed back to the hut and stared at its thatched door. A warm, rosy light glowed from within. Doubtless Woof was calculating, as always, a busy, happy man indeed. Grimoldo knocked. Slowly the door opened a peep, and an impishly smiling, squat gentleman of brilliant baldness and mildly rectangular eyes stared at Grimoldo, at which point tears rolled down Grimoldo's cheeks and a few strands of grass and bits of petal fell from his ears and lips. Woof, he said softly, I'm so glad you're here, it's the . . .

Woof slammed the door, leaving Grimoldo once more in the perfectly executed, unctuous black. The monk pounded on the door and yelled, You won't get away with it, Woof! It *is*! It's the end again! Again the door opened a peek, revealing the professor's benign smile and rectangular stare. Grimoldo, he said in a resounding bass, at least you are a correct disgrace. This was the confirmation Grimoldo had been waiting for, and he therefore concluded that he would either continue fleeing or dissolve into hysterical laughter on Woof's doorstep. As the latter course was chosen, Woof growled, Enough! It is certain, it is fated, and no one comprehends absolute vulnerability so well as you. Get up, my boy, before you turn to gelatin in your own robes!

Woof's orders were always remarkably effective, and the monk rose and entered the professor's shapeless hut. It seemed, as he registered in an involuntary scream, that even here those tell-tale signs of the end were rampant. For numberless computers spouted endless rolls of paper in a vast mechanical sigh of overwork; the paper fell into swollen, snake-like piles on the floor, and the papered floor, in turn, seemed to rise in voluptuous intimacy with the ceiling.

Now Grimoldo sensibly covered his mouth and perched himself upon a tiny stool which the professor reserved for adults of ambiguous intellectual proclivities. The old man, all the while, passed with extraordinary agility through the foamy waves of his calculations. A fish in water, the townfolk were fond of saying, a kinky old schoolmaster with his paper numbers. In fact, the villagers were fond of the professor. Often they observed him at night, driven by the uncontrollable paper out to his porch and there asleep, one hand in the doorway patting the incremental statements, as he liked to say, of the world's essential message.

Often, the paper gamboled through the doorway and collected itself in heaving, pregnant spirals on the professor's lawn. In the dawning light, the villagers could see Woof awakened by a paper curlicue tickling his nose like an affectionate dog. Thus would he sneeze and begin that act of mute intellectual wonder which revealed the earth's dawning truths, a moment perhaps akin to the beginning of the world. At such a moment, an observant villager might come to him, sit upon that splendid stool, and ask to hear the amazing tale of the earth's ongoing dimensions. This pleased the old man beyond words. It was, along with that mighty mechanism of truth within the hut, his reason for being.

Of these impressions, not one passed through Grimoldo's mind, since he was completely obsessed. His teeth even chattered as he awaited Woof's wise and friendly camaraderie. I just dunno, he stuttered, how I know but gad, I sure always do . . .

Doubtless, said Woof, truth rarely repeats itself so predictably. You are our first apocalyptic bloodhound and the end, as we know quite well, will draw us to a splendidly predictable conclusion.

Shit, I'd rather have just slept in peace, I tell you. Rather than *seeing* that thing . . .

Perceiving, Grimoldo, corrected the professor. Not all would *see* with the mind's eye, as you have done. (The monk nervously began to rub his shaven pate). Ah, smiled the professor, Superstition is unnecessary for the end is so various and subtle an experience, as we shall witness in due time. And what are you calling "that thing" for heaven's sake?

A light in the sky, until it fell, a pink one or fleshy maybe, but just a sort of flash, flashing.

Not so, Grimoldo, said Woof as he patted the monk's febrile cheek. For you alone it was a kind of darkling star, cast through an endless vault to fulfill a terrible destiny: the vanquished, utterly surrendering end, the unknowable embrace of us all by the cosmos. If it had lasted longer, you might have even heard an enraptured voice whispering, "all that is not I . . ."

But pink, sir. I swear it, that or buff, more particularly, close to flesh.

Details are inconsequential, snapped Woof. They are no more than the fruit of your nightly indulgences, flopping about in flowers and weeds and whatnot, gazing mindlessly at the heavens while your robes are drenched in the dew of earth and that of rampant, undirected thought. And now, in all your simplicity, you want action, too, don't you? You came here because you wanted me to locate the end for you with absolute precision. Woof again made that undulating, fishy motion through his streams of paper. Then he dove beneath them and came up with his own wastebasket. For me, my boy, he said, the end is nothing but the bottom of this wastebasket. Quickly! He began pulling at a strange, amorphous, pinkish mass, indeed clinging to the bottom of the basket. Help me, Boy! For heaven's sake! Woof yelled.

Both jammed their hands remorselessly into the revolting flesh and pulled for all their worth. The lump was attached with almost supernatural strength. Its repulsive contours were those of the very same The End that Grimoldo witnessed in a moment of sublime vision. Get it, get it! Woof cried. The damn thing thinks it's going to stay down there sucking on my basket! And the two men pulled, and pulled again, all the while the buff indecency, its lights flashing, began to rise hideously from the basket. Hold on, heave to! they yelled. Indeed it rose: it gurgled forth as what seemed to be an intransigent elemental force, a center of rebellious gravity, a core of the most niggardly truth, a conception made insurgent flesh. There: popping, snapping, hissing, bubbling like the crudest, most involuntary acts of maw and bowel and even, could it be? a dreadful belching croak! They both screamed as the fulsome lump at last exploded from its shell, then gleamed malignantly between their upraised fingers.

Take it! Take it! yelled Woof. It's yours, it's the meaning of your misbegotten life, your albatross. Thank god it is not mine. Now take it! It's nothing but the inveterate trash left over after my computers, my beautiful winding pages of pellucid life, have subtracted all the sublime, static truth in the world. There is no place for that wretched morsel but my wastebasket and the decadent heavens as witnessed by a notoriously unstable Vicarium monk. And the old man shook violently. Take it, he said softly, your buff creation, and let me be. For at last I must clear out all this paper and begin again. A threatening growl issued from Woof's resonant throat, a sort of Rmmwwoofm! Grimoldo knew this sound well and fled instantly, for he knew the old man to be quite murderous when his calculations were disproved again.

In the forest he glanced over his shoulder and discovered, to his astonishment, that The End was following him. There, on a branch it had gently draped its lush, flush'd, full folds of amorphous flesh, one tentacle dangling down and rippling like a question mark. My god, are you following me? he asked. Wordlessly The End protruded still another, fuller and more voluptuous tentacle over the opposite branch and absorbed it to itself with an ecstatic, suckling sound. No doubt, Grimoldo whispered, there will be much fleeing tonight. He rushed on.

Suddenly a careening form swung down from a tree and, with a hardy whallop, knocked him to the ground. He felt his head craned roughly to the side as four muscular limbs rammed him further into the soil and there, at last, did he see those cataclysmic, irreducible eyes of Natalia. Natalia! he cried, for she was the woman of his most savagely erotic nightmares; Natalia, the creature who seemed to live and breathe lust, rapine, and acrobatics; Natalia, part woman, part witch, part animal, part rubber, and part unbreakable plastic. It's all happening again! Grimoldo yelled and received in response that burning gaze, that wilderness of arms and legs with which Natalia enmeshed her prey. Again they were utterly desperate, both desirous of The End and, again, in flight from it; thus they dissolved into violent love-making for it was, above all, the most desperate act they knew.

Only a close proximity to The End, thought the monk, could justify the ecstatic pleasure they both took in one another's bruised, writhing bodies. For Natalia was capable of an endless series of transformations and was now a scarlet flower, lapping wildly at the pollen disseminated by Grimoldo's lurching form as a bee; there a female vulture, seizing the monk's talons from below and affixing them, as well as the remainder, to her posterior in a raucous flight through mountain air; now again, a predatory weasel, following a track of male spoor and ravishing her mate in an airless, claustrophic hole in the ground. And so on. When Grimoldo at last roused himself, it seemed that the sex lives of the entire plant and animal kingdom had passed before his eyes.

Natalia leaped to her feet and swung joyously from tree to tree. The monk, watching her lilting, swooping arcs about branches and treetrunks, her great leaps from grass hedges, her slight form etched darkly against the moon—realized he had no idea whether she was human or not. He tenderly examined his cuts, sores, and bruises, all the while wondering whether anyone would believe he'd gotten them as a bee. But then, surely Natalia had ravished everyone, and perhaps the last thing he needed was an explanation.

Now she was swimming rapaciously through a lake, eating the sleeping fish in a train of foamy water. Then she was devouring birds, bales of grass, for her jubilant nature could go no longer without food than without sex. Shortly she would return . . . Grimoldo stared at the heavens, for there was no more escape from Natalia than from The End. And how was that fleshy pink polyp taking it all? The monk glanced about himself and was drawn to a loud sucking noise at the base of a tree. The End was bubbling away in ecstacy, sucking up trunk, branches, soil and grass at once. Grimoldo thought of one more unfortunate than himself—Woof. For Woof and Natalia . . . but that was still another nightmare.

A flock of birds flew out of a thicket, pursued by Natalia. She shot straight above them in a leap, bagging the six highest at one throw. What efficiency, Grimoldo whispered . . . and I'm next. After Natalia had finished devouring the birds, she flashed a savage smile to the heavens, raised her slender though formidable arms, and leaped upon Grimoldo. Now the monk was pinned beneath her, and he stared with mute fatalism. Take me, he said, a Vicarium monk has no will. He marveled at Natalia's slenderly efficient form, capable of so much appetite and so much plunder.

But of course, he thought, Nature may not have created her. Perhaps she was a daughter of The End. Or was she Nature striking back with a vengeance? But then, Natalia allowed little time for reflection. He was quickly embroiled by a sulphurous gaze, by animal sparks in flashing eyes, and her language, a fluid warbling sound she uttered throughout every moment of lusty attack. Her face grew larger and wilder as she bent toward him, gently scraping his chest with her deadly fingernails. Oh it was happening again, whatever one called it: bloodlust, violence, sex, love or The End. Then: ants copulating, toads copulating, dandelions, possums, dolphins, flies, anything, anyone else copulating. Natalia could manage it all . . .

The next morning, Grimoldo found himself in a small pit. It was the spot he had occupied with Natalia, but the ground had sunk several feet. She was gone, leaving the monk to painfully force his beleaguered limbs out of the hole. As he finally rolled to level ground, an agonizing cramp in his knee reminded him of the tarantula's intricate mating dance.

Now he was up, staring at the last sunrise, the day when it would all pass away, even Natalia. All the lust, all the plunder, he whispered, monasteries, wars, computers, even all the fear and trembling, even me! Nothing but nothing coming up. Inexplicably, Grimoldo felt a surge of energy. They'd all have a fine time of it today. A holiday! A festival, wasn't it? At least he sauntered through the forest at a slow, appreciative pace and looked about himself with satisfaction. There was reason enough. The End, at last! You just couldn't stop yourself from feeling rather delighted. A smile cracked in the crevices of Grimoldo's painfully abraded cheeks. Time to let go . . .

So the end came, and it was a honey. It fulfilled all apocalyptic prophecies projected by scientists, politicians, and religious crazies. All were gratified—for a moment. The earth boiled itself to a lovely, fine vapor, then recrystallized through the most awesome processes to a gleaming snowball, thus adhering exactly to the predictions of everyone. The Great War was fought, and each downtrodden nation was pre-eminent and uncontrollably aggressive for five minutes, until vapor fuzzed out the edges of all conflicts. Reported present were a lake of fire, a large wine-press, and an enormous icicle shaped like a bolt of lightning. Just before North America was consumed by vapor, the east and west coasts did break off and sink into the ocean, as had long been expected. The sunlight, too, was in fact blotted out by petroleum pollutants as well as the War's radiation. Thus the earth rapidly froze all the while that the poles were melting from combustion. Several moments of the long-awaited Fourth Ice Age therefore occurred, and the surface of the continents was ground away, up until the moment when they exploded into vapor. Domesticated and wild animals were wiped out in equal numbers, and the same was true of religious fanatics and deviants, thus confirming the last-minute prophecies of both.

All survivors were hopelessly crippled monstrosities, until genetic damage caused an irreversible beautification of all bodily parts. Thus the New City of a perfect world order was born upon earth, at least until the ideal justice of its denizens proclaimed humanity as culpable for the apocalypse. Sacrificing themselves to their greatest enemies, the arthropods, the perfect citizens were justly devoured. Rule of the arthropods had long been prophecied and equally prophetic was the notion that aliens would interfere with earthly life. And sure enough, the strange behavior of the earth was noted by aliens who decided to inject superhuman intelligence into the arthropods such that they didn't destroy themselves. In the absence of self demolition, however, entropy took over and caused a natural degeneration of arthropods back to the relatively minor level of human consciousness.

Thus did humanity survive.

But what was it like for those astonishing individuals who had known all along of the apocalypse? What was the end to those whose vision extended to the horizon of themselves? As mentioned previously, it was a honey. So we return to the monk, who at this moment is once again running in panic, for the forest opens up behind him and emits a great, feral roar. Natalia vaults through the trees, delightedly catching then dropping the feisty young men, and following her is an explosion of flesh: all the filth, fun, lechery, rags, rage, and half-nudity of the raucous Middle Ages. Through trees, leaves, and hedges are desirous, half-opened eyes, round red lips over numberless gap-teeth, tongues waggling, great bulges of flesh beloved and unveiled, every orifice and extremity open to dazzling light. The villagers are hanging from vines, crying out in predatory bliss, diving into vats of ale, stout, and mead, rocking the bushes with pandemonious acts. Most frothy and outrageous are the monks and even (Grimoldo fears) Mother Primora, for her rocking chair has been abandoned as well as her imposing black gown, now lying tousled and free, upon the forest floor. Grimoldo averts his eyes in abject politeness. And above, round, and through he sees the polyp itself, village-sized and lunging. It has expanded to enormity while rolling over the ecstatic villagers, crunching the monastery to shards, aimlessly tossing the crumpled bits of Woof's computers—altogether, a tide of besmirched joy.

Grimoldo was relieved to see Woof in one piece. There, in the distance, the old fellow wandered about with a lost and distracted air, sniffing flowers, apparently speechless. The monk rushed up, grabbed him by the shoulders and exclaimed, The Dark Ages are over, professor! We're Modern!

The old man oriented himself with a scowl and replied, The Dark Ages will never end, my boy.

But then, we must have returned to them, and still the end is nigh. History is circular! That's what it all means.

Simplicities, answered Woof, generalities. Circles solely exist on paper, and this is clearly the one event I do not tabulate.

Curvilinear, then.

My young friend, you mean semantic.

Rectilinear! cried the monk. The old professor stared in astonishment with that hauntingly rectangular gaze. A strange, distracted smile played on his lips.

No comment, he said, and wandered off with two daisies clutched to his bosom.

And Natalia? No words at all, Grimoldo thought. If The End was the moment's circumference, Natalia was its center, igniting it all in a flash. Here, there her warbles, her strange gestures seemed not incomprehensible but totally communicative, too intimate for words. She was the source of contact within the noisy throng; thus were they singing, exclaiming, declaiming, enflaming; consorting, vehemently denying, crying, plying themselves so completely that, at last she became a tapestry of eyes above them—and there they seemed to belong, on the earth, receptive.

Then Natalia's greatest transformation shook the ground. It seemed to the villagers as though they fell through a shaft between vertical and horizontal perception. And falling, there fell away from them a lifetime of vertically upright, entrenched sensation, where distinctions and divergences were sun and water to the world, where stability pushed upward and lived, inevitable as plant life. Veering off to another plane, they molded themselves upon the horizontal—elastic, fluid, charged. Natalia's theater spun with dialectical motion, herself the ideal, opposing partner to any transformation. Here, in this floating horizontal frame, there emerged that occlusion of fear and desire known as revolution. The villagers were becoming all classes, races, revolving genders, multiple species, each twist in the self ignited by Natalia as partner in opposition. Thus were they visionaries to scribes, royalty to serfs, prophets to followers, avengers to destroyers, immortals to bleeding mortals, fire and ice. In these transient selves was expressed want, hatred, violence, bereavement, unspeakable plenitude. All they had ever feared and desired merged in climactic images, and in these shining reflections was portrayed a progression of life: The prophecies passed before their eyes and their forms resounded.

Then, as suddenly as it had begun, the spell ended. They were villagers again, milling about a festival, and it was the end. As a finale, Natalia fell down vengefully upon the poor old professor. Such unequal combat seemed too shocking to watch, but no one moved. Here was Natalia's most bizarre transformation. As Woof lay on the ground, it seemed as though he were a peering, sniffing, ferreting creature, justly made for minute, erratic motions across the soil's surface—a digger, a plodder. His round, bald head began to expand while his appendages shrank and circled, in sinuous motions, toward that bulb-like head. Like a crab! to its carapace! they exclaimed. With this great, moist bulb, rufously glowing over sturdy little pincers, Woof was the very picture of taut, scuttling crustacean life!

And no more had the old fellow altered in every part than Natalia kicked him about the forest as though he were a soccer ball. To the villagers' astonishment, Woof seemed to enjoy the game as he held his tiny crab-like limbs stoutly at attention and rebounded, in small though distinguished bumpy-jumps, to any insult kicked into him. Grimoldo and the villagers were fascinated that such plucky forebearance lay in the old fellow. A cheer ripped loose from the crowd. To which Woof—in glowing, blushing, springing sphericity, and limbs clenched evenly beneath his chin—responded with a grin! With a last kick, Natalia wandered off into the woods, leaving the villagers to rush up and congratulate the heroic old professor. As Woof's head and limbs popped back to normal, he blushed a deeper shade of pleasure and humiliation. Thank you, thank you, he said breathlessly. This was his finest hour, and he knew it.

After such revelations, Grimoldo found himself wandering distractedly into the forest. He looked for Natalia, but could find no vaulting, ravishing, or brutalizing going on—very odd, he concluded. As he reached the forest, the din began to recede. He looked up at the sky, as was his habit. It had darkened rapidly, or they missed the sunset. Or rather, they were the sunset. Or rather . . . or even . . . His thoughts, intolerably profuse earlier, seemed to straggle out and end in silence. In the sky he saw the stars, now pin-pricked and harsh—rough, edgy things like cold breath sucked in, foreboding. Foreboding! he cried and began to move about nervously, an idea hatching. There in the sky—a difference! Something gone . . . Yes! Why, the stars had sucked the earth like a raw egg! Not a change on the surface, in the eyes of things, not a sign to read, but . . . a new order, a new state of energy itself, a new cry on his trembling lips. Then came that fearfully prophetic, inevitable sound. Winding out as dully, as repetitively as a machine, he could hear Mother Primora's rocking chair creaking away, back and forth, forth and back . . .

It's starting again! he screamed and rushed throughout the villagers. The crowd had been still and silent for several moments so his wild movements were unhampered. It's begun already! he shouted again. They treated his announcement as an echo to their own fatigue. O.K., they shrugged, he's still the best and most obnoxious bloodhound on beginnings and endings—sure enough. Never were they so conscious of his social deficiencies: the filthy, bare feet; the appallingly huge, round eyes, ever open in panic or wonder; that oddly shaped, shaven head and above all, those mothy words from a dry mouth.

Mother Primora now snored deeply and, for an instant, she seemed to be accompanying the monk in his repetitive cries. That was it. The moment crumpled in upon itself like a used napkin and was done. Woof sat on the grass mumbling to himself: Flesh . . . flesh in spite of itself . . . Bone, tooth, hair, blood, toe.

Only the edge of Natalia's gown was visible as she disappeared into the forest. Take me with you! Grimoldo screamed. But he stopped. No one could ever follow Natalia. She came to you instead, rarely, and only when she pleased. Now, thought the monk, now she would make love in great, green throbs to leaves and grasses;

wind, sprout to the torsos of trees and love them; recline in waves and ravish water-lillies; weave shining scales and twine with reptiles; then warm her, soft her, to wooly fur and love with mammals. Who could say anything about her, except that she would leave?

In the quiet dark, the monk could hear Woof continuing his recitation. Lip, the old man stated decisively, toe, tooth, hair, blood, bone. He repeated these items in different serials, then frowned as their significance continued to elude him. Grimoldo did not interrupt him. After all, the night was empty. And this, this beginning—it was simple, austere, stark, rigid enough. Fear and desire were only a memory, anyway.

Grimoldo wandered back to his nighttime post in the weeds and felt the returning dew upon his feet. As for The End, well, that was done, through, finished, *kaput*.

HOLOGRAMS, UNLIMITED

THE HOLOGRAM ARRIVED so quickly. That was remarkable, first. Marian and Jonathan said to one another, "But we just thought of it! But we hadn't even decided!" and laughed knowingly, as though someone were entertaining them in secret. They were accustomed to being covertly entertained; their intuition always selected the most subtle, unexpected, and intriguing novels, plays, films, journals, dinners out, overseas vacations, one-year leases, and postage stamps. They spoke in unison; that was the second remarkable thing. They were both exceptionally sensitive to one another, as they often observed, but they had never thought in unison before.

"I did think you wanted it though," Jonathan said tenderly.

"Well, I thought you did, but I wasn't sure, myself," Marian said helpfully. Many new things were acquired in this way; for Jonathan and Marian were, as they often observed, a highly educated, highly intellectual, childless, upper-class couple whose ages and professions placed them in the highest spending group of statistically represented Americans. The leading edge, they once said, in exploring, demanding, in sensing vividly, in bringing it all back to their apartment. Before marriage, or consolidation as they once confided, they were known as John and Mary, but many compromises had been made. Secretly, Marian wished that Jonathan had been named something more penetrating and incisive like Christopher, but she said nothing and, since Jonathan wished that Marian had been named something more elusive and intangible like Erica, he said nothing either. Above all, they knew they were lovers—lovers and tasters of a strangeness and succulence to life—and not entirely spouses though they had of course consolidated. Now they smiled at their penchant for experiments involving one another. After all, they were the first generation to pass entirely beyond consumption of status to consumption of mind and the senses, they thought, almost consumption boundlessly, in itself. They could play with life, they had that type of pure courage, and they had each other. Two is wonderfully extravagant, they thought in unison; then so many remarkable things began to happen that they never bothered to count.

There was that irresistible note from the hologram company. It said something about the hologram synthesizing all equipment emitting electromagnetic energy into three-dimensional forms. Now this was both exciting and practical, for they did have so many things—movie projectors, stereos, a vibrating bed and aquarium set, an office ceiling computer pendant, a gallery of superb surrealist paintings framed with nite-lites in the garden for late strolls, prints of their last favorite theater performance which twirled slowly upon a plexiglass disc bathing everything in a fluidly changing color, mauve at this moment, etc. Drawing things together—why, they hadn't bought that, had they? "I can't recall it," said Marian.

"Not until now," Jonathan said tenderly, and neither noticed this time that they were thinking in unison. The note—on an embossed card, like a polite greeting—said that they would have direct sensation of everything in their immediate environment. "Even of you," Jonathan said.

"You, too," said Marian, "we'll be snug." (Both were too highly informed not to realize that their own brains emitted electromagnetic waves.) But the machine, they thought, the machine was now strangely familiar, and they still had no idea how it had gotten into their home. Jonathan suddenly suspected faulty workmanship as the machine unconscionably began to resemble a pair of crumpled and dirty jockey shorts he had just left in the bedroom. Marian thought she saw it wink lewdly.

"At least we haven't really bought it yet," Jonathan said. "It just turned up. It dropped by—nothing more. We can still pack it back the way it came if there's any horseplay here." That made them feel more at ease. The word, *horseplay*, had allowed them to rid themselves of a number of unpleasant things, impossibly frustrating moments when they bought something they shouldn't have.

Along with the greeting card, the hologram was accompanied by a folder describing some of the "feeling-tones," as it said, that could be chosen. A string of titles appeared which included Protozoa, Black Hole, Minority Report, Black Navel, Violence to Violins, Elemental, Woman, Quasar, Revolution, Mankind, Beginnings and Endings, The Joker is Wild . . . and they stopped reading. "We can just tastefully choose anything we want," Jonathan said tenderly.

"I know," said Marian brightly, "just like before," They kissed and then when they both happened to think, "I wonder what Protozoa . . ."

PROTOZOA

> Warm-pool-dark: eyeless. Reaching to a bound: pulse. Soundless. Reaching, expanding, growing up to. Minute flickerings of sun-touch, spaced through. Wobbles. Contorts along a line a lever: two now. Two touch sides and flow the whole. Ever once like a ring the thing and so divide: four now. Once upon a light they go: and go.

Marian and Jonathan looked furtively at one another and both said in unison, "I'm afraid I . . ." and then, again, they knew in unison. "Of course we were thinking Protozoa and then the machine . . ."

"Turned on . . ." from Jonathan.

"Or was . . ." from Marian.

"Or made them . . ." from Jonathan.

"Or we did . . ." from Marian.

"They were, that is," from someone.

"Oh definitely, they were just here," from anyone.

"Here?"

It was becoming so difficult, they thought, to finish sentences when so much was being thought so publicly, and thought in unison, so difficult to finish them, the thoughts. Life dangled exorbitantly.

"Exorbitantly, you think?" asked Marian.

"Protozoa," Jonathan said with finality. Finality felt wonderful. "Oh wonderful!" responded Marian. "That's what that business was."

"I didn't like it," someone said. This was followed by an embarrassed silence. Jonathan and Marian could barely look at one another for each, they thought, had no idea which had pronounced judgment. It was so serious, so inflexible, so plainly terrifying to criticize a new media appliance. Suddenly both brought their heads together and whispered in unison, "Do you realize we've never done it before?" And then, "Nothing like that again or . . ."

"It'll hear . . ."

". . .the hologram will hear us. . ." Whispers, everywhere whispers, strangely like angels made of kleenex, an ad and a vision crossed, drifted and fell, fell and drifted, all about the room.

"It even made those whispers," whispered Jonathan.

"Certainly," whispered Marian, "we'd never think whispers like that." Or did we? Jonathan and Marian glided again, or so they thought, up to the boundary between themselves and the hologram. Marian suddenly decided it might be tactful to say something nice about Protozoa. "I suppose," she said, "we're swarming with them anyway." Almost . . . but then, with It here, who's swarming with whom, she nearly . . .

Jonathan, with a keen effort to summarize from experience: "You can't expect much from white noise."

Marian, eagerly: "That's right, of course, they're just white noise."

"So of course someone made it into an art form."

"And then it just turns up one day in your living room."

"And you may not like it, but it's only a matter of cultivated tastes, and there are others who . . ."

". . . and others again . . ."

"We even knew that one before we were thinking in unison."

". . . and the white noise people will like it."

"The ones who made it . . ."

"I hope they're not protozoan."

A very long silence ensued. It was finally broken by someone: "Frankly, it was the most senseless thing I've ever thought." A pause, then pauses (of pauses), pauses as thick as whispers and as dreadful. I have, thought someone, a definite sense of something ominous, something encroaching . . .

"You think it's encroaching?" said Marian.

". . . I was afraid . . ."

"Yes, I know, it's the hologram, it's doing everything."

Don't! Jonathan thought in agony. I don't want any more damned feeling-tones and we can't, we just can't think!

Don't blame me! thought-cried Marian. I didn't think any more than you did!

And put away that folder of titles or God only knows what we're going to get next! yelled pure, disembodied thought.

Mary thought, perhaps even said, That's it! Don't think! But unfortunately their first impression was something like Why me? and so—

MANKIND

> I think it is the mournfulest face that ever was painted from reality; an altogether tragic, heart-affecting face. There is in it, as a foundation

> of it, the softness, tenderness, gentle affection as of a child; but all this is as if congealed into sharp contradiction, into abnegation, isolation, proud hopeless pain. A soft ethereal soul looking out as from imprisonment of thick-ribbed ice! Withal it is a silent pain too, a scornful one: the lip is curled in a kind of godlike disdain of the thing that is eating out his heart, —as if it were withal a mean insignificant thing, as if he whom it had power to torture and strangle were greater than it. The face of one wholly against the world. Affection all converted into indignation: an implacable indignation; slow, equable, silent, like that of a god! The eye, too, it looks out in a kind of *surprise*, a kind of inquiry, Why the world was of such a sort? This is

"Who?" demanded two hot bristles of infuriated thought. "Who is that!"

BYLINE: Thomas Carlyle

To their astonishment, it ended in hysterical laughter. John's thought nearly screamed, My God, that was worse than Protozoa! Mary agonized in laughter, Oh, it was! It was! suddenly: Don't! in thoughts-clipped. We're thinking again. Don't even mention Protozoa or we'll get it again and I don't want

PROTOZOA

> Ink-drop-night. The nearly leg'd, it moves. The way to live interiors, sun-bowel'd. From heat-heart to rim, beats the source; makes

another, its mirror of time: barest of outline, shading, motion, change. It orients to the light.

Stay calm now, thought-saying-said John. I think, well, the best way of putting it is: this is at present a hostile environment. We have no idea

How it started, exactly, thought-continued Mary, but some form of pollution has been activated in our living room

Is here, that is, thought John. I entirely agree: this is simply an instance of environmental pollution. We know these events represent a very low problem

Probability, corrected Mary, thought-thinking-out. But it can happen to anyone, and we'll simply

(We've thought *simply* at least twice now, counted John.)

We'll just ride it out, that's what we'll do. These things have happened to others

An inspiration: others of what? thought-bled John (for he had pressed his fingernails deeply into his palm).

Don't confuse me, thinking-still Mary, especially with blood. It's simply that

(3 times counted . . .)

We're not unique and have nothing to fear . . .

O.K., thought-bled John, hand me a bandage, and we'll find our place in this mistake.

Oh, our place, our niche! laugh-thought Mary. Oh my God! Our little hole, in this very home, in my own . . .

Don't become hystrical! shrieked someone. Hand me a bandage and shut up! And don't use vague words like *hole* or we'll get that

BLACK HOLE

I. *Preliminary finding*: beyond parameter of Milky Way, a collection of cohering primeval genes, originally from Earth. They are approaching a black hole. (Spot check for audition: "Summit of all epic quests," uttered by one "astronaut." Translation imprecise in historical diction. Stop: await further request/information from terminal.)

II. *Probable context*: last historical instance of subjective, descriptive language, one century prior to conversion into alphabetic and numerical indices of equivalence or personal request. "I need you": A + B = AB. Translation again imprecise in then-current diction. To terminal: supply opposite? Does it appear in another early synthetic equation? Awaiting further development.

III. *Sequence*: "astronauts" are diving into the black hole like (request for metaphor clearance) a bunch of guppies. Initial sensation: their fingers are expanding. One "astronaut" states, "a gigantic, an unearthly reach. . ." Response from other astronaut, "not unlike (request for second metaphor clearance) the human instinct to pursue knowledge." Appears to be an interchange. Parties have peculiar grimaces on their faces. (Request clearance for interpretative facial allowances—is this a "snarl"?)

IV. *Method of operation*: utmost care and attention has been given to this, though event itself is of no consequence. The information contains the dangerous "light dirt" paradox which necessitates our use of the ancient verbal method of representation. We must presume that the astronauts comprehend nothing, since their position is indeterminate in all dimensions. The ancient verbal form encodes atemporal, nonspatial images; that is, nothing at all. It is therefore possible to categorize it in its own terms and, more importantly, destroy it such that there is no further loss of efficiency in the terminal.

V. *Final spot check*: one of the "astronauts," a young woman named Alice who made a hobby of ancient linguistics, is heard to mutter involuntarily, "curioser and curioser."

Awaiting determination: operation is complete.

Clearance: paradox is apprehended and event may be removed from our universe of probability.

—What is this violation of all secrecy, normalcy, decency, diplomacy, efficiency, relevancy, rest? —Careful with abstract nouns! It does these terrible things with abstract nouns! —What is this violation of all nouns? (Has it come up with a verb yet? —Don't give it any ideas. It does nothing but eat up and blurt back ideas.) —But what does? —It's a virus. It's attacking the genome, engram, and sensorium at once! —What a horribly viral virus. What antiquated expressions. —The worst, the worst. It's converting us into our own mental images. —My words, we have no defenses. —Only our mental images of defenses. —And that's even worse. —But we must stop it! We owe it to ourselves! —You mean, our mental images of our self-referents. —We owe even more to them! —Yes, yes. —I know what you mean. —Oh good, then I know what you mean, too. —No matter, *it* knows. —Then we'll all know in a minute.

IT KNOWS

My engrams of genomes, sensorium
decided to hold a moratorium
and so they declared
they were full of hot air
and thereby became my new hologram

—That's vulgar. Limericks are vulgar. —I knew we were vulgar. —And furthermore, do we believe it?

M-A-ARY! gasped, brayed a voice, barely human. O-ohh! softer, a whoosh, scarcely sounded . . . John!

Oh my God, Mary, are you there?

I think so, I really do.

Brief, wobbly sense of fingertips touching, delicious: you really are there. And then: his boyish haircut, his even row of teeth, his rumpled suit attesting to much aggressive protest, a flailing of arms at least. And there: had she ever looked so lovely? Her exquisite, gently curving knees bent in the air, her relaxed and supple limbs, the stare only at him, the hair as wispy-soft as . . . something said milkweed. Why milkweed? he thought. Why not? thought something. Well, milkweed, they agreed. He reached out to embrace her and found his arms passing entirely through her clavicle and shoulder blades.

"I don't care, darling. It's you. . ." Her arms went straight through his biceps, Adam's apple, and dangled on the other side of the wall.

"We'll just be grateful for what we have . . ."

"We've only lost a little matter."

"And might have lost so much more, just imagine . . ."

Swiftly, he kissed her mouth shut. And then: never more instinctively, more spontaneously, so like children at heart they tore off their clothing, cascaded jackets, stockings, buttons, zippers, shirts, skirts, pants, briefs upon the upper walls, and missed copulation by a hairsbreadth, for

CHRISTOPHER AND ERICA

He: for it began with her fascination. Unlike any other man she had ever known, but all she had imagined. No tender vagaries of youth yet never a harsh line of manhood, not a hint of callousness yet never a lapse in pellucid, cosmopolitan knowledge of the world, never a slip, a dip, no need to aspire for he was the pinnacle, the dancer, a light, luminous shadow, barely corporeal yet doubtless rippling with moist, slightly tensed muscles. Defined solely by negatives and superlatives, the not that, never this, ever before, she held him in cool pursuit down endless corridors, breathless, pursued, dreamed, dreamt, negated again and again, engendered, invented yet more superlatives: stalked, stalked, stalked.

He had of course done great things. Even the odor of his skin smelled of boardrooms, bedrooms, money, safaries, fame. She could never specify which for they revolved about her like fountains, stars; and he, in his utterly knowing way, never spoke a word of himself. And then his finely molded face with its flickering, impossibly subtle expressions. Oh, he made her quite frantic and, in contact with this pure incandescence, she developed a morbid fear of forgetting him entirely and thus hastily wrote the word, "Christopher," on a piece of paper, to be tucked away in her wallet for safekeeping.

She: not like any other woman, but many glimpses of perfection. That hint of the Amazon in her svelte height, that incommunicable center of sexual renunciation, nonetheless, he was as certain of as the finely tuned tendons of his heels as he bent toward her. Her face was as ineffable as a wind of petals and so her voice, gestures, throat, her slender arms, reaching, reaching. (Had they ever touched? But of course they had. They had had sex. Hadn't they?) He only thought "Erica" and all erotica resounded. For that was their greatest mutual delight—the locations of their lovemaking. The walls, vine-covered, wine-rippled, would wheel like light-maddened suns and never remain one thing. Perhaps it was a stream or brook for tenderness, a rooftop for daring, a bear rug for irony, an altar for delicious fear. And it was that, it was just that—the impossibility of definition, crystallization, the fading of walls, trees, spires, shades into one another, the whirling, the gasping. For in fact they did gasp more and more and louder and faster. Christopher and Erica, above all, could never quite get enough breath to reach satisfaction as they tore, gasping, perspiring and never could, never did

SPANISH EYES

Whereupon, and impetuously, exultantly, into the room burst Spain.

Spain was aggressive, enormous, domineering, not to be put off; moreover, full of bulls, wine, candelabra, glinting knives, bloodred skies, liquid joys, bulls and more bulls.

—Whose disorderly imagination is responsible for . . . he began.

—I didn't, I swear . . . she began.

No! cried Spain, for *I* am Spain! I summon myself and then . . . I magnificently go on summoning.

They would have gazed at one another in horror, but they had no eyes. For Spain, and Spain alone, was everything. And they marvelled at Spain, for he did not move but in vistas, panoramas, the rockiest, the fiercest terrain rushing skyward, a test of strength at every cliff, mountaintop, then avalanching downward, did she, into boulders, plains, numberless lives gloriously snuffed out; at last cities, avenues of such enormity, such unbridled lust they themselves said cosmopolitan; she never spoke but in profusions, dispersions; he did not love but in water, sunlight, pouring, sparkling, wrenching, ringing, reeking, she was above all, with sweat, alcohol, saliva; shrinking in a flash to twisted alleyways, tiny rooms shaped of smoke, deadly decisions, greed, infinite sex, every inch illegal, contraband, all of Amsterdam in a plain brown wrapper, ballooning with consenting adults; he was ceaseless, inevitable, she was reckless, uncompromised; he, irresistible, she, insuperable.

Come to Spain, said Spain, in the most mellifluous tones that ever blotted out the world, where life is cheap: and sex and death, the most expensive in the world.

—Don't we want it the other way around? someone asked.

Not now, not now, grinned Spain: brutally, promiscuously, joyously, politically, economically, neverendingly.

That's why it's here, someone said.

When you're in the middle . . .

. . . of an orgasm . . .

. . . it's always Spain.

They had, some moments before, stopped breathing. One must, one thought, do something, at least put it into words.

He viscerates, John tried.

She does, Mary agreed. They wanted to do just that. And then be rid of Spain.

But then, Spain could be more Spain still. Spain could be egregious, intolerable, a bandilero of outstretched nerves. Then it was reeling, rippling, dripping, rushing, Spain was nought, nothing but motion; falling, singing, bloody banging, I can't stand. . .

Neither can I

we've got to stop

Spain!

I have an idea

in the middle of this?

really, an idea

we go backward and change the

the, the?

one that came before. . .

CHRIS AND ERICA MAE

He was leaning against the side of the motel office, waiting for her to knock off work. A seed was caught between his teeth from dinner, and he tasted it again along with beer and tobacco. It all mingled pleasantly with his memory of her body. She locked the door to the office and walked around the corner directly to him, though he'd given no sign he was there. "I can always count on you, Chris," she said and thought, You're so damned dumb you couldn't think of another thing to do. The only thing that surprised her was the fact that he already had the blanket out of his trunk and slung over his shoulder. He tugged on it aggressively.

"All we need, Erica Mae," he said. He knew his eyes glittered rather fiercely before the motel's red and white electric bulbs. She laughed. They didn't say much more, never did. Every so often, he called her his dumb broad. Then she called him her dumb truck driver. There didn't seem to be much difference until the blanket went down. And the blanket went down. It was all so clear, simple, and fast. Especially fast. Suddenly they'd notice the wind rising and the sweat covering them. My usual solid job, he thought. And what else would I want a bozo like him around for? she thought, and ran her hands over the grass clinging to her thighs.

He rose and put on his pants. It made him feel really fine to leave the shirt off. "'Night."

"'Night, Chris." Sometimes he left first, sometimes she did. It didn't matter. Suddenly he loved the fine puffs of dust raised by his own heavy boots in the dirt road. It was a good thing they had, no bullshit. They got just what they wanted. He thought of her back there, lying so still. Instantly, he gauged his satisfaction and found nothing wanting. Then he remembered—they'd gone off the blanket and into the wet grass. Now he thought about the dew he had seen running down the side of her thigh lying there, in the grass. She was like that now. Perhaps she shivered, liking it. Well at least, he thought, I might have taken a bit more time at it.

Afterplay or something. When she rose, her thighs would be covered with moisture and imprinted with night grasses. It was nearly as though she were turning into someone else, unknown. Naw, he thought sheepishly, Chris doesn't think things like that. He walked on in the dust and felt the heavy tread of his boots.

They found themselves on the floor again, their clothing scattered all over the room. Something was definitely over and done with. John looked at her nervously. "Did you have an. . ?"

"Yes," she said emphatically. "Several. Your usual solid job. You, too?"

"Yes, several." He was irked. "I'm glad I wasn't too much of a bozo."

"It wasn't us."

"Just our bodies," he said.

"We certainly used them, whoever they belonged to."

"Do you feel all right about it?"

"I just feel so damned relaxed," she said. "I don't care about anything." She did look wonderful, he thought. "How are we going to get rid of that machine?"

"I don't know." They laughed and said in unison, "It finally did come through with some advantages. . ." and again, more seriously, "But not really. . ." They both looked away. And back together, "You know." "Oh, yes!" they answered.

"I thought I'd try talking to it," she said.

"Talking?"

"It talks to us."

"It's more than talking, and furthermore, we're doing it."

"But that's just it—we're quite reasonable and we can just leave ourselves alone."

He was speechless. "I can't think of an argument against it."

"Neither can I," she said. "And we're polite and compassionate enough, as people go, so we'd do it for someone else and we're nearly that, too, aren't we?" Again, he could think of no objection.

Go ahead, they thought. O.K., it decided.

She stared at the machine for a long time. It won't mind staring, they thought, it does so much of it. We'll stare some. And what was it like, anyway? It was a machine, of course, they knew that, a vaguely metallic little box-thing. But then again, it was something like gravel, somewhat like oil, strangely like bird feathers, like tree trunks, like gaping, distant summers, plumbers, flummers, flim-flam, alakazam, oh, my God, stop!

"Stop!" she yelled, and was fairly certain it was she who yelled. "You may be anything I think you are, but that doesn't mean I don't have plenty of complaints." They all waited with anticipation. In fact, anticipation was breathing audibly in the room, was wheezing with effort, with irritation, it was, after all, something like flim-flam, something like alakazam, No! Don't go backwards! "John," she said and again was quite certain it was she speaking, "It's too distracting to keep my mind on my mind."—I know dear. I've tried not to confuse you with all of ours.—Thank you.

And again, in the loudest, clearest voice clearly her own: "You are not like us. You don't belong here. Find some other universe to inhabit." She didn't see her husband gesticulating wildly behind her. Mary, no, that really won't work . . .

For it was utterly false, they all knew it. The machine was too perfectly like them, that was the difficulty. And falseness was everywhere, believe us, everything. The floors, the walls were unspeakably artificial. Numberless musty, taxidermized animals leered out from gold-plated frames, and the lies of our childhood were spoken in fierce whispers from their formaldehyde lips. It was false, ungodly false, and suddenly all the baroque and rococo in the world spun hideously into the room like a vast, triumphal pink layered wedding cake!

"Oh, please," cried Mary. "It was only a little white one."

Oh please, please please, echoed baroque and rococo savagely, for things spoke here, they spoke to you and you to them.

Just get out! Mary screamed. Just leave us the-way-we-were-before! Just leave us alone.

Alone! The cake was gone. Spain, baroque and rococo, Jonathan, John, Chris, everyone had cleared out. She looked about herself in alarm. It was so shockingly alone. The vacancy swept from room to room, trembled delicately upon the non-furnishings, gazed in glassy blindness from the non-windows, attempted to press itself almost painfully, almost erotically upon what was not, never could be, ever again. And it was just this trembling, this pitiful timbre of the air halted in motion, nearly a sound, a never-wailing for what was desired and desired profligately . . . Alright! I've had it. Be done with it. Come back, damn you! And the room was flooded with John and Johns arriving by floodlight, footlights, bringing home little hologram machines by the multitudes and fast upon their heels were all their new found friends, Spain, Black Hole, Protozoa . . .

She fainted dead away.

FORGETFULNESS

I will forget it, I know I can still forget . . .

Mary, you're babbling. You just fainted, you haven't been able to forget anything. None of us have.

"I don't know about the rest of you," she said distinctly, "but I'm forgetting," and fainted dead away again.

How did you manage that? he asked. Dead away and everything?

She barely rose again, bleary eyed and said, Just clearly, vividly, imagine fainting. It's quite simple.

Their insensate heads hit the floor at the identical moment.

For life was renewing itself, after all. . .

The quantity they could forget was astonishing, until they forgot it. It was not even so much personalities or individual histories; they had forgotten at least a century, perhaps more, for their means of comparison was silent as well. Oh, they'd gotten around it, they thought, that thing happening before. And before. . . when the future was before and the past to come. . .then they were free. Freedom was much simpler, too, for no one in the past had come close to remembering it yet, at least not by the standards of those who were enslaved by the future. No one had been defined, dominated, for the sense of it was registered in the future, and rendered in the past. The past, ongoing, palpable, was free. There were no upheavals yet, no theories of violent change, nothing to retrieve and nothing irretrievable.

And an edge, an edge of a hem. Attached to a very long skirt. A simple one, made of rough cloth. That was the first thing she touched. Then she raised it to her nose, smelled it, slowly (slowly), registered her amazement. Nothing like this, ever before. She rose to her feet and felt firm, well exercised muscles, skin with the sun-warmed odor of being outdoors for many hours. Where? (in delight). And there he was. A broad brimmed hat lay on the table, and next to it he sat in thick, loose pants of a similar, coarse material, a collarless shirt, a vest, shapeless and worn, and tall boots. His hair was long, uncombed, much brighter. And he was cleaning a rifle which lay across his knees. He looked up at her and smiled, then returned to his work. As amazing as it all was, he did not feel the need to describe it, to probe her for a reaction. He was completely occupied—intent, engrossed, calm. Suddenly it occurred to her that he would not make so much of her, would not always be watching her, obsessed. The observation passed away without any further need to interpret or analyze. She was absorbed, too. Her hands were moving rapidly over a wooden object which she recognized as a picture frame. She was joining two segments of wood together at the base; the wood itself had been stained and buffed a short time ago. When? She was entirely adept at the task without any recollection of its sequence. It was all so astonishing. She placed the frame beside her and looked up again. The walls were made of logs, a single room, yet lighted by a flickering of candles which, in the waning daylight and darkness at the corners of the room, left a sense that it expanded slightly. Over the fireplace, which was filled with rough timber, stood a photo of someone they recognized as the President of the United States, yet whose name they could not remember. The time was far less striking than the sense that it was continuous, engrossing; they were absorbed by it and, thoughtlessly, they were happy.

She walked to the window, which had been unshuttered and stood open, without glass. The air, blowing in to her, was clear and soft. It was dusk. She must have lit the candles sometime before and, she reflected, that was early, for the candles were precious. So she had been here some indefinable time before she became aware of the edge of her shirt, a moment ago. And then, looking out the window, slowly (for it happened slowly now), she noticed the greatest change of all. It was the way in which, she thought, she became aware of space. Space was the forest, the length of the clearing and its splaying out, like a hand or a shell, before the cabin; a particular fullness, a roundness of the trees before they broke into the sky and darkly pale distances, the sky above. There was a way that she simply let the sensations occur without interpreting them, a way she felt a part of what was visible, known so well. Space was where you were in relation. She knew the forest at different times of the day, different seasons, as well as she knew her husband's presence. And the clearing—it was something they had made themselves, as well as the cabin. That was the difference, in terms of which space had reorganized itself: they were a part of that, what they could always see and remember, looking upward. Upward, the sky was space, and tangible, present, too. When they looked up, they were related through all the fibers of memory, body, and action; a kind of living thing, a kind of tree or garden, below the sky.

Before (and she could remember clearly), space was the apartment or the street. It could nearly vanish when she was absorbed, leaving a hot lightness, a palpable nothing with noise, a red inside the head. And it expanded into unknown distances and forms when she was intensely aware of it. The apartment was endless, space she could count to herself in steps yet not get out of. The street was a winding concrete wall of sound, motion, intrigue, something she could never know well. Upward, the sky did not exist or if it did, it was a kind of reminder, a memory without content, so distant it was not a part of the world. If she thought of it, she felt even more locked into motion at eye level, into space that expands in receding. Now, it was this other space, expanding on contact, which meant something she called, unable to remember the other words, spiritual. She turned to John. Did he see this, too?

At the moment, he was conscious only of the gun. Or rather, he continued thinking, the motion. Or the entire act, ongoing, the way he finished it and then began again. The application of the oil, the movement into the barrel, the sweep away and out. As much, what it would be used for. The necessity, the simplicity. It was that so absorbing him, an astonishment as great as what his wife was now sensing. He had never completed anything of which he had been so totally aware, which so became the world. It was only and entirely the substance, here, on the rifle, its gradations and effect, the movement into and around, the heavy feel of this necessity upon his knees, in his fingertips, the sun in the morning when it would be used, the air, the medium of its use, the offering. That's what it was, that's what he was doing. There, in the clearing of the forest, which he knew as well as his wife, the rifle existed in and of itself. He moved, he was—in relation to that, the things making up his life, now. She was using that word he could not remember. But the clearing, the forest, and the sky above—these were the facts. And the cabin, his wife, the rifle, his coarse, shapeless clothing were in and toward these facts. The word scarcely muttered but the action itself was space, the thing she was thinking of.

He looked up and placed the rifle on the floor. He wiped his hands and finally joined her beside the window. Together, they watched the dusk grow darker and the trees close out all the fine detail of daylight. Then the forest was no longer a manifold collection of living facts, a green city of forms, but the dark simplicity of a uniform presence: towering, sentient, faintly ominous, inhuman. Their eyes moved away (they could not look at it for long), up to the sky, languorous and full of distances in its blue, finely and impossibly alive in its beginning starlight. Then it, too, grew dark, occluded space and vision the way the forest had, made a single statement they could not read except that it was not human. The clearing seemed to move closer, though it had lost its detail, its life, the multifariousness of all remembered things. It was desolate, limpid, gentler than the sky. Still it remained in relation: it was where they lived, in and with this world that so slowly opened and closed.

They opened the door and walked out into the clearing. As the forest drew closer, there was less occlusion. The trees formed dark striations into the sky, which was still a great, black door, closed. They were directly beneath a huge, heavy trunked tree, and it began moving in the breeze as everything—everything—opened. There was nothing stranger and more beautiful, they thought, than this tree at night. The lively green city was gone, the world branching to a commerce of lives beyond their own. At night the tree was all of life, the life itself, the life beneath, beginning. Space, then, was the dark, rippling leaves that were never still, holding and reflecting life in continual motion, the leaves raising themselves into the world and the sky as one; the trunk, branches, a primordial base to this upsurging motion, and the expanse overhead, drawn close: as perfectly an embodiment of space as they could imagine. For it must have this base, must rise up and proliferate to branching implications of its rise, and then the liveliest, the most turbulent growths waving beyond. This was all of space drawn perfectly into relation, entirely alive. A tree at night, they said. There were other words, some which seemed imperative, but they forgot them. A spirit, they said, but the meaning was older than the word. A tree at night, they said. That was enough, that was it.

They walked through the clearing again and sat in the grass beside the cabin. Soon they would be back inside, their hands moving over the tasks they had set for themselves. But now, the light flickered out from the candle, made their shadows and clothing move, and they wanted more of the flickering, the motion, upon them. At a distance, the trees of the forest drew together again in their vision and collected, were silent. Animals, or leaves, stirred high in the forest, creating undifferentiated sound. Suddenly the dark, the flickering of light, and quiet were something else, too much. Only the clearing was lucid, memorable. The rest seemed resistant to them as they watched. They could make no more images of it, and their own silence was passive and dully inhuman, like the sky's. A sensation of pressure grew as they sat still, unable to speak to one another. It was then that the forest and the sky began to exert a tug, a power; it was almost fear they felt. But more, they wanted the strange pressure to break, for the reservoir of silence, darkness, space, to be filled with something of themselves. The space, the space that had transfixed them, barely began to rupture. The clearing was no longer the prelude or focus, the forest not the rising up, the border of their world, the sky rushed in, yet it was empty: it was all shifting about, nearly reversing itself.

They waited. They listened.

It was then that they saw a figure coming toward them, out of the forest. They were amazed at the length of time it took them to notice. By the window, she would have seen a change in the forest's darkened network long before he was visible. Now, he was nearly upon them, part of the shifting focus. He. A man walking with a backpack. A wide brimmed hat as he approached. Someone like them. They were not afraid but for the disruption, the disproportion. A broad smile, even, a wave of the hand, a hullo, glad to see you, folks.

His tone of voice, something like a salesman. But then, it was all over—space was the cabin, huge in its flickering, its unknowability, and the man. They rose from their silence and knew they would talk to the man for hours; the space had been set. "How-do," he said. "Name's Andy Jackson Turner." A large, red, rough handshake. A man from the frontier, they thought, a traveller after his fortune. They welcomed him in, offered a bed for the night, a meal. Andy Jackson Turner expected all of this but was nonetheless appreciative. "You're doin' me a good favor, folks. I've been on the trail for days on end."

"You must be one of those frontiersmen," said Mary, attempting to sound sociable, "who's going to change the West. How is the West, anyway?" Andy Jackson Turner stopped in the middle of the cabin with a bang of his enormous boots.

"Did I hear you right, ma'am?"

Suddenly she realized she'd forgotten what she did remember. In embarrassment, she began, "Of course we've read. . .we've heard about such things from time to time, even hereabouts." He still looked startled. "Other travellers, like yourself . . . we hear some about what they call the West." He grinned broadly and sat down. Now you're talkin', lady . . . now he knew she knew something, or at least that he deserved an awfully good meal and bed.

"Right, ma'am," he said. "We've all got our little plans . . . I mean, our great ones." But he was strangely ill at ease—he looked at her sidelong in a cagey fashion. What was he thinking, the loud oaf, she thought. He looked over at John, who had closed his eyes in utter disgust. Mary . . . he seemed to say . . . a whole evening of this?

A stay-at-home, a loafer, thought Andy Jackson Turner. Nothin' for history.

History! thought John, at which point Mary's historical imagination produced a cornmeal souffle and a venison steak. Andy ate it as though he could improve the world by gobbling it up.

He's really kind of innocent, thought Mary. Yeah, thought John, by God, he doesn't know much. They thought again of the future, the one they escaped. "Well, Andy, what of it?" Mary said to the man who clucked and smacked like a man, as only a man could who felt the world expand beneath his fingertips, grow tastier, more succulent, boundlessly. It wouldn't take much to get him going.

He hadn't even heard her question. But the stay-at-homes always wanted to know the big plans of the ones out tearing up the plains, he knew that for sure. Poor folk . . . if only they loved life the way he did. Prodigiously he smacked, like creation itself. And he was all ready on big plans. But first, he stared at them in that curious way, as though he'd actually hold something back. They were expecting a fugue of boasting, louder and wilder and wilier. But he was silent, as though he, too, expected something. Oddly impenetrable he was, John thought, for such a simple, predictable man, a cartoon they'd read about in grade school history books. Andy smiled silently in his cagey way and looked out the window. "Plans are all in the works," he said. "You folks make that little clearing?"

"Sure did," John said. Still this strange man had not tried to glorify himself. What was he waiting for? Andy Jackson Turner just swilled away at his dinner. Why didn't he combine all his pleasures?

Mary thought she might just prompt him a bit. "So . . . the West, eh? Boomtowns, horses, gold, gambling, railroads . . ." She realized she was remembering too much and stopped. He looked at her in suppressed astonishment. She knew a mite, he thought, and she wasn't talking. That stay-at-home did, too. That's why the little snip was pretending to be bored with it, things damnably more important than him.

Andy Jackson Turner ate on righteously and said, "A clearing, huh? You ever dream about clearings, cabins everywhere and planting forests, instead? Just like gardens?" This was real, it was the future, but very odd for the past, they thought. Was he like them, someone from the future, too? But no, they decided, he was just, simply, too crass. The real past, doubtless.

"No," said Mary. "Is that your big plan out West?" He'd nearly finished his dinner now and dropped a pipe and tobacco from his pocket.

"Ain't nobody going to play with that one yet." At least, thought Mary, I hoped I might be able to figure out what year this is. And he keeps giving us that sidelong stare. I hope he's not dangerous. What does he want to hear, anyway? Suddenly he was on his feet and fidgeting in the bag, then he drew out a collection of small bottles with poorly printed labels. "This is part of my big plans, ma'am," he said. Mary looked back at John, but he was trying to pretend he'd fallen asleep. Oh, alright, she thought, I'll listen to him.

Bottles, strange ones, were all over the table. One looked like a fat little chimney atop a bowl; another was completely rectangular but for a lopsided cap. All were asymmetrical, filled with unattractively colored liquids, pasted with hand printed labels containing generous stains. She felt as though she were being introduced to a bunch of dwarves or broken toy soldiers. She picked them up gingerly and suppressed a laugh. "There's at least one for you, ma'am, depending on your heart's desire." He had them all upright now, though it hardly mattered, and he stared at her intently. His face, rigid in its grimy roughness, looked like that of a furious tyrant, forcing his midgets into a circus ring. He seemed to sense her surprise and amusement. Then he hunched forward aggressively: "You ever think, honestly ma'am, you'd like to have real big, soft breasts that dangle like gold watches?" John's chair, which was tilted back against the wall, fell forward with a crash. "I got salves n' emulsions here that'll give you just about that, believe me, straight from the best scientists back east."

"And you, young fella," continued Andy Jackson Turner. "I'm glad you're up and awake now, 'cause I got plenty for you, too. Got a little bottle that'll keep you going nights. And another that'll grow a real beard on you. I never heard of a feller out here without a beard. I expect you might use a little on your chest, too." John was up on his feet now, glaring at Andy Jackson Turner.

It was so gross, well, there was no point in saying so. He put his hand on his wife's shoulder protectively. Don't be afraid, he thought, a harmless numbskull out peddling early American well water. In the forest too long, horny. I'm not worried, thought Mary, it's wonderful.

Andy sat down proudly, leaving all his mythical wares on the table. "Now you folks just sit down again," he said. "I've said a mouthful, I know." So he's the host now, thought John, with all his asinine arrogance. He said nothing and continued standing. That strange smile played across Andy Jackson Turner's face. "Well-l-l," he said, "I reckon I got you folks' attention now. Yes, you damned ass, John thought.

"You was falling asleep and you, ma'am, was touching those bottles like they was old cow flop." He seemed to be getting at something, for all his grossness, thought Mary. All considered, they were both thoroughly interested in what Andy Jackson Turner was going to say next. Still smiling, he looked like he held a fine poker hand. He snapped his suspenders rhythmically, like a ringleader summoning ponies, and watched them with silent satisfaction. This really is too much, thought John, and sat down next to Mary. This guy's an awful bore, isn't he?

I wonder if he'll break his suspenders, thought Mary. A con man is pretty fair at building up suspense. Then Andy took out a handkerchief, wiped his face pensively and thoroughly, moved it to his back pocket where his fingers came back with a toothpick and, rather than putting it in his mouth, he frowned at it for a few minutes, turning it about all the while. "Oh my God," John said audibly. Andy looked up and tossed the toothpick away. Then, in one brisk, dramatic gesture, he swept all the bottles off the table.

"You thought I was selling you them bottles of stuff, didn't you?" and he roared with laughter. Mary thought, They're tough bottles, not a one of them broke. What on earth is he doing? A lively, paranoid gleam shone in his eye. "I could see you folks knew a little bit 'bout the West, people like me. So I'm gonna talk to you about what's important, 'cause you know a little and I know more!" Now he glowered at them, silently thundered; his suspenders positively click-clacked from the rapid motion of his thumbs; the bottles glittered unmistakably, even leered; he was going to talk, to shout; they wondered whether he was violent. He rolled his sleeves up and made his hands into great, fisty wads. "I'm gonna talk to you . . . about what? Do you know?" he yelled.

Hell no, thought John.

"About religion!" John and Mary both expelled a generous breath. No, he was not going to attack them, he was a harmless nut, after all, no frontiersman, nothing of history. A kind of horny bum, John thought, wandering around alone. Mind a bit addled. To their all too obvious relief, he countered by banging the wall and smashing the photo of the President of the United States. They were on their toes again, watching him carefully. O.K., an authentic madman, they thought. "Religion!" he cried. "Of the people, by the people, for the people. So they don't perish from the land nor be no wetsops. And you folks know it."

"Ah, no," said Mary, and found her voice quavering. "We probably don't remember, if we ever did read about it."

"Read! You *know*, folks. I've been seeing it *in* you, in your minds, ever since I walked up here!" This had a familiar ring. But anyway, he was making it up, that or hallucinating and furthermore, these religious people had to be shut up or they'd become violent or violently boring; everyone knew that. "The religion of the people." He paused and solemnly sweated like a pool of grease. But these religious people could sweat, they thought. "Of them, for them, the one they made up themselves!" He pulled the shutters open, let the night wind blow into the room, and snuffed out the candle. They were on their feet instantly. This was utterly unexpected. It was almost pitch-black, then lit by the moon. The clearing seemed to have blotted out the scene; it was huge, amoeboid, yet plain, without markings, unrecognizable. It seemed to expand at the window all the while the man was a stark, angular shadow in the dark. "Look at that out there, something you can hardly see." In the shading of the moonlight they could see disgust on his face rather than violence, glistening with the sweat of righteousness. "Nothin' out there." He seemed to make his point only to undo it; then his heavy, checkered arm swept the room. "It's all in here, isn't it, the room." His fingers came to rest on his temple. Naw, thought John, not much in there . . .

"There!" shouted Andy Jackson Turner. "You bet, folks, I'm a frontiersman. I been on both coasts, I seen all that's in between and more, I seen the light." They were waiting for the light, and in the meantime, John slowly moved the rifle up to his knees. Take no chances with a nut, even the harmless type . . .

"We matter, that's religion! We remake the world—in our own image!" A dead silence, the crux, his point made, and all energy seemed to leave the man heaving for breath. Well, I've got my rifle, anyway, thought John.

"Where are we?" asked Mary out of the black. "What year is it?" It was all too familiar, suddenly.

"Our own time!" shouted Andy. "High time we stamp ourselves . . . on that!" A checkered arm pointed out the window.

"I can't see anything," John said.

"You bet you can't!" yelled Andy. "So you ever think what it'd be like to have it all lit up out there, whole towns all lit up and going for miles and miles and what you see is us. That's it, boy, that's religion!"

"It isn't any time, is it?" said Mary miserably. "It isn't the past, is it?"

"You bet it ain't. We're striking right out for the future, ma'am."

"Well, we don't remember it."

"No, we don't," added John. They tried to be as firm as possible.

"My God, you folks . . . " said Andy Jackson Turner. "My God, you're weird."

"You're a real potboiler yourself," said John. "And if you do anything besides shout and throw bottles around . . ."

"That's right! said Andy, remembering his bottles. "Now them bottles . . . there we got a deal." He tossed them back up on the table in the dark, as though he remembered the size and weight of every one. "You may not be good enough to buy religion, folks, but anything else your hearts desire . . . is bottled up right here, waiting to be unstoppered, like God's rain. Cleaners, softeners, hardeners, colorizers, bleachers, dissolvers, hair for your head, blood for your toes, love, wonder . . . "

"Now see here," shouted John. "We're not buying a drop of your damned toilet bowl!"

"That was something, young fella. I never heard that one before."

"And you just move along out of here, too." Andy Jackson Turner was silent, and still. The moonlight revealed nothing; he seemed to be headless. A shirt came out of the dark and receded back, a red coal in a pipe glowed weakly, went out. And utter silence, but for the pipe mechanically returning again and again to the table. What on earth? something thought. Where am I? What is this man to me? "I meant now," said John, and his voice had lost all force. What on earth were they up against? Was he going to stay forever, like that machine? Was he? "I meant you leave now."

Andy leaned forward, puffing and headless. "Folks," he said softly, "I think we ought to pray together. I'm a gonna pray right here out loud and you follow along . . ." For an instant, they thought they would do it, automatically, repeat the man's words in the perfectly blank moment he had created, a headless stone carving words on itself. No one knew whether the gun exploded first or the lights came on: it was all rush, flash, and a new world outracing smoke. The apartment reeled into view. We're back, thought Mary. Why . . .

I shot him . . . "Mary, I shot him!" John said. "I couldn't stand it anymore."

It doesn't matter . . .

I know . . .

But I also feel terrible that we're back.

It doesn't help much. But it wasn't any better in the past . . . finally.

No, it wasn't. The space of the apartment seemed enormous. How long would they wander here, now? On the center of the table was one of Andy's bottles. It was filled with a black liquid, and unmarked.

"It's one of his, I'm sure of it," John said, astonished. "The rest of them are gone, the ones with labels. Is it ink?"

"No, it's the solvent."

"Are you sure?"

I was watching . . .

I wonder why it's here . . .

We can use it . . . She turned the bottle around in her palm. It was hopelessly contorted and opaque. No light shown from its surface, and dust covered every inch of it, as though it had been sitting on the table for years . . . longer than years . . . She dropped it. A filthy accident, it was, and one from another world. Well it had failed. They had. Life was entirely memorable. She couldn't recall when she'd felt so despondent and her memory, at that moment, seemed flawless.

They looked around the room. There was nothing else to do but gawk at fate, they thought, like bums, like pigeons. Their home, all clear, planed, dull surfaces, a heaven of order itself, and the machine, still in the corner of the room. Ongoing, they thought, like all of history, like that indistinguishable time they called the future, a myth, a cradle of light, a forever-thing. A very odd sound came from John's pursed lips, a scratchy-sketchy noise like a broken record. He'd be the first to break, Mary thought. He always did if he didn't hover about her, husbandly. She watched him, expecting embarrassment. And so it was. In a flash he was down on his knees before the machine, asking it: are you God?

And that did it, that really was the last straw. If she had to maintain the only sanity in the room . . . and wasn't that the way of it with men, time and again? Always regarding themselves as more courageous, exploratory, philosophical, aggressive in reaching after the unknown? And what did it amount to here but reverting to the Middle Ages, monks down on their knees? Oh, she could have kicked him. This foolishness in the face of that sly, revolting piece of metal and whatever undreamt of else. And how the machine would use him, how it would mortify them both. It was no partner for dialogue at all. It was nothing but caprice and even a bit, even an edge, of the demonic! To trust it to answer a question, to attribute absolute knowledge to it—why, she could hear its hideously clattering-computer-metallic voice say, "The information is incomplete" or some such thing. A snub from a machine, next on the list no doubt. Instead

Well there, she thought, you have it. Are you satisfied? That machine is totally unpredictable except in its capacity to unnerve us all. It's God in a valentine—are you going to stay down on your knees over that? And before he had time, even, to think through his wife's anger, another question popped out of him: are you our savior? And before anyone had time to take it back

THE INFORMATION IS INCOMPLETE.

She closed her eyes, she just blotted it out. At least one real or imagined human being was not going to be undone by this thing, not going to ask unreal questions, drop down on imaginary knees, do all of these impossibly paradoxical things that made the mind, the real one, reel and reel about for something to hold onto

ELEMENTAL

> Myself, and a flight. A dive through blue-auguring space, a dream of clouds outraced, land-looming-loving, earthsphere and home. A beauty proximal, birdhigh and blue-beholding, closeness to ground. You can fly: she flew so. Close for the sweep, a love in it, closer. Now over the leaves, the flowers, round of a melon, sun-leavened flare in up-streaming air. Quick breath of higher, impossible playfully, prayerfully, birdhigh and windlength, worldly empyrean. Now tawny the sun-like, winding the torso, on air, of air, beauty an even so closer to earth. And far. Turning the winding, the shaking in air, there treetops there grasses, the restless cloudhandfuls, the water its foam-swells, the flowing, the pauses. Begin again. Begin. So full of rainswept, measuring clouds-gap, widening flight for a taking-embracing. Then floating afar, cloud for the reaching, tree for green-roaming, wind in its rushing: now dive for the sun.
>
> Flight. Beautiful thing in its floating, comes after, thing of beauty. Yours.

She was moved; she heard herself say it. She was at rest, still tingling from flight, touched and moved to the very quick. There was a sense, infinitely rare, that she had indeed a core, quickened; and something had reached it, soundlessly and completely. Nothing more was needed—it was felt. Her anger at the machine had long since evaporated. Why? in pure wonder. Why did it do such things, placing revelations and absurdities side by side? What sort of thing did this? What sort of thing was it? "I," she said aloud, "have had a religious experience." It didn't surprise her. Nothing did now. Life lapsed supremely, like an ocean of one's own. Nothing entered her mind, nothing at all . . .

. . . constriction in the shoulder, a cramp, rub it away of course, she came upon . . . "tall wooden chair," she said, marvelled: "Blank screen.

BLANK SCREEN. WITH CHAIRS.

And it was. She was undeniably sitting on a straight-backed chair, which generated the discomfort in her shoulder. There—it was rubbed away. Now that screen: they were sitting in a large auditorium, watching a blank screen. Or so she assumed. He was beside her, utterly absorbed. He pressed her hand to acknowledge it, but did not take his eyes off the screen. It seemed to be a theater house, but there was no visible projector and nothing on the screen. How long . . . fruitless. The machine moved both forward and back in time. She removed her hand from her shoulder and noticed, almost as an afterthought, that she was naked . . . "Naked," she said aloud—it was rather

NAKED ON CHAIR.

pleasant. Why not? . . . steadily increasing sound . . . absolutely. Why, the room was full of people! And how slowly all these sensations came to her when they were simply where one was, one's position in space as felt . . . How quick and fine this perception had been before. Before? Sometime, at any rate. Other couples were sitting in theater rows. "Couples!" Absolute

COUPLES, COUPLES.

repetition—couple by couple by couple. "But of course," she said aloud.

INEVITABLE.

She watched them. A few, animatedly discussing the book of hologram titles, were fully clothed. Most were naked, like herself and John. That was right; she felt certain that was what should be happening, whatever it was. Some were like John, oblivious of all but the screen. Some seemed to be unconscious and slumped over one another like . . . "like muffins,"

MUFFINS.

she said. And then they were muffins. She quickly turned her eyes away from them in embarrassment. Had she been like that? Had someone made something amorphous and ludicrous of her? She turned and frowned suspiciously at the couple behind her. Or at least, it had been a couple a moment ago. The woman was now gazing in wonder at a bear beside her who was, in turn, frowning suspiciously back. Well, it would all pass . . . But how had she been? Doing what? She stared back at the screen and was aware she had instantly called it "blank screen!"

BLANK JOHN.

He turned his head slowly and looked at her without recognition, his eyes travelling about an invisible rectangular space in the air. "No," she said, "that's the screen. I'm Mary."—Oh yes, he thought, thank you for that illumination . . . there are so many and one is grateful . . . She nearly shivered as his hypnotized eyes travelled back to the screen. Obviously, he was, it was, well . . .

JOHN'S OWN SCREEN.

She turned away and began thinking about herself. "Naturally," she thought. What's else to do here?

She stretched out and considered, momentarily, the new . . . future, it would have to be called. The one with the machine, well, everywhere. Now she couldn't locate it by sight but then, the metal model was probably outmoded. That's how these things went on. And so the machine, invisible as visibly everything, moved on to the future, its future, theirs. And would she continue to be Mary, after all? For one could peek at the future and see the most amazing transformations. Yes, she was Mary. Of sorts.

In fact, she began saying to herself, the oddest part was that they had planned so ingeniously for the future. Really they had, the leading edge and all; they were none other than the spearheads of the future. It was a favorite topic of conversation. You could bring it up with anybody. And now with any thing, too. They were certain that the sole direction of human life was one of proliferating and more awesome change, each alternative generating not fewer but surely greater and greater alternative designs of the world to be. Once, during a game of charades, they speculated that the word, *decision*, would drop out of the language entirely, for choices, such as they were, became fibrous networks instantly growing from stems that just as swiftly disappeared. It was an hilarious moment, she recalled, trying to pantomime a reverse order of the plant and animal kingdom. What had they done? Stood dictionaries, tables, roses, themselves—on their heads? For, in the future, what would animals and roses have to do with it, with life? The future was laden with capice, phantasmagoria, that was the future.

So you see, they were prepared, she was thinking. Perhaps they would be the first generation to utilize genetic engineering, the last to age, even to die, the first to be rejuvenated, who could say? And then it might be so intriguing to be changed into other species, other essences entirely. To be the first, yet, to create an emergent form of the environment or even to transform perception of the world as though it were a game of permutations and combinations. Maybe permutations and combinations would replace charades, really, she thought. More mystery, more fun altogether. There would be games in the future. Games, games, games, games, games.

But then, you know, she knew, one had to be prepared for terror. How odd terror was. After all, who would be the last recognizably human voice sounding before, and who knew? an unlimited expanse of perception, the destruction of space and time? Why are *who* and *what* separate terms, she thought it thought . . . And then blunders! blunders so in the midst of it all, the future. Perhaps, they once said . . . and keep tabs on *they* she said, it makes its thought go on . . . and . . . perhaps blunders of cancerous races, species, civilizations, journeys to an infinite nowhere. And could you, all of it, be ready for the moment when such consequences would be indistinguishable?

"Arms, yes . . ." the arms of the chair steadied her. But they were, why, even beyond that. The verve, the leading edge. They were prepared, and best so, to relinquish themselves to the future, to welcome it. They knew that the issues—political, scientific, metaphysical, moral—were what we should, could be; what the world must be in the midst of alternatives which, singly, were multiplicative. They understood that science, politics, literature would confront these decisions. And they wanted, above all else, to be the first generation to regard them as outmoded. And now, that was all very sincere, didn't it think so? Now the hologram was here, the thing, she said "that made change itself relative," it was saying, wasn't it? and a momentary distraction in which she became John Donne in the seventeenth century, a sonnet composing itself with a lacy hand.

"Or," a man beside her (did it think it was her husband?) continued, "that anything that happens, may be happening in another shape of my mind, or hologram, and not here, or in other holograms, other versions of me," and a brief distraction in which he was swatted upon his ear, the ear belonging to a Japanese monk, his roshi glowering above him with a switch. Neither bothered to think what, specifically, was happening, but the distractions, they thought, the distractions were life itself. —And it's happening so concretely that I know nothing except, it really exists. —It's that we've created the world in our own mental images.

For they knew, imageless, the mind's pure incandescence: miraculously reflecting its own processes of life, severing itself from terrestrial origin, possessing an unlimited capacity to evolve in its own terms. Multitudes, multiples, multifarious, multi . . . she was saying, hypnotized. They knew that adaptation to such a process was the one and only fact. For they were the creatures, above all, who did this, who were this fact; the future's compulsion was irrevocable. And they were also the first generation to love an ever receding horizon of themselves; and a momentary distraction in which they became James writing "a house of cards" becoming Fitzgerald writing "the furthest evolution of a class" becoming . . . But they relinquished it. All of writing was obsolete.

They had invited this phenomenon to come into their living room for an evening's entertainment. It arrived on time, guest-perfect, another layer upon the fact, reflection of the reflection, the very energy of incandescence. Was it a machine, hologram, themselves? And they knew it was none—both older and newer than these, a metaphor come tingling with blood. Still another distraction saying "incipient life forms," careful, protection of "law . . . international . . . intrapsychic . . ." It came slowly and was instantly obliterated. Scientific and political responsibility were hopelessly obsolete.

"Inevitable . . . Final." In all its caprice, life was so like that.

You were just sitting, after all, before the screen. Then you became one of its images . . . recall the first one, she was . . . that odd little . . .

PROTOZOA

Overland, underland, moves in the round. Home of air, touch of green, on a stone, in the

> bones. Being true, never knew it. Little bit of sun and it's gone.

Now she paused over this strangely complete, rhythmic life process, so unlike themselves. Maybe Protozoa was the best of the lot, really. For them, it just picked the new sequence. "Picked?" It passed her hands through her legs—there was no tactile sensation at all.—What is *it*? it asked. The next hologram? The cue word? —The future, he answered. Still another splice of its moment. —Do you mean to imply choice? it asked again. —You just pick, she heard herself say it. Like pick a wart, pick a cabbage or an apple, pick a sore. Stick out your fingers and

> As though pressing a button or, if that's too mechanical, a rose from a stem but—inevitably—

PICK.

THE MAN WHO TOOK A BITE OUT OF HIS WIFE

LYING BESIDE HIS WIFE after making love, Eric smiled at his own wonder: given the passion he felt for Karen, his wife, why hadn't he devoured her many times over? Yet here she lay—a lovely, breathing burden of flesh. Then, his impulse somewhere in the velvet chasm between thought and reality, where whirl those soft, hypnotic creatures of the mind who long so dangerously to be, his desire hardened, became real. He took a bit of skin between her breasts into his mouth, bit neatly, and swallowed.

Karen ran her finger slowly down his cheek and paused at the mouth. This hole had sucked her into its world. Eric was gray suddenly; the muscles of his face were pitted, stone-like, and his mouth was a moist cavern, teeth hovering in shadows, within. Behind the shade, in the room's half-light, they were a strange, colorless terrain to one another—a suddenness of flesh cliffs erupting, valleys subsiding into wild, pooled tangles of hair, a tide of liquid breaking remotely on a shore. The air seemed full of beating wings, rapacious beaks. Their mouths had the deep, mineral taste of blood.

They had been married for eight months. The bite had been anticipated from the beginning of their relationship and now that it had come, it was as familiar to them as the shadows in the room. As Eric began to sleep, he felt the weight of his body and the lightness of breathing more acutely than ever before. He felt simple, natural; now it was safer to sleep and dream. Karen touched the spot between her breasts where her husband had eaten and felt nothing at all. This startled her, and she realized how much she had expected from an absence: a flood of impressions about herself and her husband, a reservoir of feeling, a mystery, wholeness, touching ground, rest.

Beyond a doubt, there was nothing new in bed with her but an absence of self. Yet this absence was hardly a nothingness. It seemed alive and willful. It could push or prod her, change her. Perhaps it already had, for here, now, she had a fierce desire to gain something. And gain she did: behind her eyes, rippling over the world, was a distinct change. The room was warped in some way. It was as though the room were present with a distorted double-image. This was enough for Karen. She would decide just what she had gained in the morning. And so they slept, deeply, as though a painful conflict had been resolved.

When Eric awoke, he felt a surge of energy. He knew that he had profoundly enriched his marriage, that both he and his wife would be immeasurably happier and more content with their life together. He thought of other men and pitied those who lacked this passionate commitment to their wives. He had always known that feeding upon his wife was the actual purpose of marriage; if he had doubted, procrastinated, it was only a doubt of his own hunger, whether he would ever be quite hungry enough to take his first bite.

He thought of Karen's radiantly accepting body throughout the morning at the architectural firm where he worked. The company's largest project for months had been a waterfront building restoration which would recreate the nineteenth century harbor. He was responsible for generating a series of computer simulations which would model various dimensions of the waterfront's eventual use—traffic flow, merchant trade, impact on aquatic life, etc.

He had often seen his work as artificial, skeletal, unimaginative, and viewed himself as one of the company's lesser lights, perhaps ineligible for advancement. Today, however, he and his work were transformed, redeemed. He did not exist, after all, in relation; he was the man who is nourished by his family and whose work is its product. He was therefore no more a chaser of probability's phantoms; he was producing the earth's finest, truest work. He looked at the day, streaming in refracted waves of sunlight, and for an instant remembered how he had envisioned the sun as a child: molten, radiant, pivotal. This summer day was a great, yellow horse on whose back he rode, alone. A thread of drool escaped from his lips.

When Karen awoke, she instantly touched the spot where the bite had been taken and wondered whether she would always wake up with this thought. Then she lay very still, evaluating the warped visual surface before her eyes. The room definitely had a double-image now, she decided. There was the room as it had existed and another room, suffused by a white light that made everything look vague, unreal. Or, on the other hand, was the other room not a distortion but somehow an intensification of the original room, highlighting what was sterile, clinical, brutal? She could not decide.

In the morning, she generally painted or sculpted for several hours, broke for lunch, then painted throughout the afternoon. For three days, she had been painting a still life composed of fruit, a dirty, crumpled pair of gloves, and a dead rose. Now, as she looked at the still life, she saw two completely different scenes. There was the still life as she had seen it earlier but smaller, remote, almost two-dimensional. The contrast between the fruit's ample roundness and the finely desiccated surface of the dead rose had intrigued her earlier. The gloves lay comfortably wallowing in dirt and moisture, a bridge between poles. Now, the scene looked mockingly inconsequential, empty, the gloves an afterthought.

In the second still life, nature was running riot: the apple was a magnificently round, red jug of plenitude; the banana was trumpeting, insinuating; the gloves grabbed, desired; and the rose! The rose was heaping fibrous layers of an exquisite cobweb, a deathliness that spun, draped, spawned, overwhelmed.

Then she heard a sound. It was a kind of burbling, like a clogged drain opening—one of the kitchen's raucously reassuring sighs. Feeling very light-headed, she walked to the kitchen and found, as she was now beginning to anticipate, two distinct kitchens. There was the expected kitchen and another filled with the ambiguous white light which, as she looked, almost seemed a semantic state: was the room emptier, less real, or was it fuller, more definite, even harsh? In the second kitchen, she saw a gray mass beside the drain. It was emitting the burbling guzzle she had heard earlier. The strangely diffuse sound, coupled with this shapeless, bubbling form made her feel she was in the presence of something obscene. An obscenity is living in the drain, she thought, and wondered whether this thought could possibly be hers. The creature burbled and sighed in what seemed to be recognition. "You're hungry," she said, "but I won't feed you. I want you to starve." Then she walked from the second kitchen to the first to the living room and sat before the fruit.

Now, she discovered that it calmed her to hold the fruit and enumerate each item. This is my fruit, she thought, this apple, this banana. I must keep them for my family. And this lovely dead rose, which flakes and dissolves in my hand, is for me alone. She felt the weight of her possessions, her gains, almost ecstatically. Yet painting was now dangerous, she thought. Which room, which still life, would she paint? Which interpretation of the room would be allowed by the vindictive white light? Yet, she was growing more comfortable. Her gains, after all, were awesome.

Karen closed her eyes and saw a young child, as round and plump as a pink porcelain jug. She could feel the fine hum of its growth; skin, muscle, blood were coursing through it, making it larger every moment. I must feed it, she thought. I will give it this fruit, and then everything in the room—brushes, paint, canvas. Such a beautiful, hungry child.

She could not possibly paint today, she decided, and walked straight out into the street, her smock mottled with paint like drops of blood. Then she entered an endless, over-lighted, roaring room: a supermarket. She felt confused and light-headed but knew she could not stop. The spot between her breasts was leading her.

Many women were in the supermarket milling about with their children. Most of the roar was composed of these babbling children, restive carts, the hum of manifold divergent purposes locked in a rectangle. There were no men beyond a few employees in white aprons with ragged, bloody stains over their sleeves and abdomens.

She stopped before one of these men, who stood beside a cart, placing organ meats on flat pieces of styrofoam, then covering their surfaces with transparent wrapping. He was a slenderly hardened man of fifty with wizened, knot-like muscles and side-burns jutting low over square, pitted jaws. Hypnotically swift in his movements, he wrapped a dozen cuts of meat as she watched, periodically wiping his hands, making claw-like streaks down the white apron. Then she recognized what had caught her attention. A smile played at the edges of his dry lips and as he wiped his hands, a white mass rose between his thighs. Yet he continued, oblivious to her, packaging organs and now lividly gleaming cuts of beefsteak. As she stood before this man, she realized that if he looked up at her, she would do anything he asked, even lie on his tarnished cart, open her legs to him, and feel the deep, harsh pressures of his maleness. More claws spent themselves down the front of his apron, and he never noticed the woman standing before him.

She tore herself away and plunged deeper into the store. The overhead light seemed so perfectly placed that there were no shadows and all was as it would be, she thought, in a desert. No shadows, just these women, children, carts, moving spasmodically. They were the women who fed their husbands, like herself. She could perceive these women so clearly now—those painfully refined, over-finished expressions on their faces: something had been devoured around the edges. They were such small, delicate gifts rising out of chaos: diminutive appetizers, exquisite puddings, delicate pink liquids rising through a straw to trim, masculine lips. How carefully they covered their edges—folding them over, tucking them up, tying them gently, pinning, sealing over the holes, the craggy edges where something had been devoured, lovely dolls waving goodbye, goodbye, for they were all receding, vanishing in so many languorous bites of living. She passed a row of tiny, glinting cans and nodded to them.

How pleasant it was to be this lovely, tarnished woman, walking straight through a supermarket. The warping had mysteriously vanished. She was a woman looking at the world with the new, shining eyes of a doll.

It was a half-hour before she reached the subway and could vanish into its square, grimy mouth. Below, the bowels of the earth were rumbling, groaning for her, and the cars arrived and stood still before her like a row of huge, blackened teeth. She waited, breathing in the rich, excretory air of the subway—curls of smoke, tar, and urine—the city's black breath and anus. Then she rode back and forth on the car throughout the afternoon and thought of the apple being squeezed, back and forth, through the city's entrails. So were they all—the passive riders, reduced to one spot, one weight, shifting back and forth in the city's massive digestion. Here the warping was gone, too; here she was at peace. Knowing that no one would watch her, she opened her legs, and a delicious band of pressure began to roll between her thighs. The car shifted abruptly beneath her buttocks like a man's hands—rough, thoughtless.

When she returned home in the late afternoon, Eric was there. He grabbed her abruptly from behind, and they made love uncontrollably. Yet, he did not take another bite of her. She prepared dinner in a voluptuous heat of expectation. Eric watched her from the dining room, his eyes grave and black. They ate in perfect silence. When they next remembered, they had become the naked gray terrain in the bedroom's half-light. She saw two husbands, two rooms. In the second bedroom, where the air was hot and pungent, she at last felt the deep, heavy pressure she desired, and he took one bite after another—she could not count how many. In the second bedroom, her back and thighs still arched toward him.

They are asleep now, and the dark encloses them. Eric awakens for no reason, he thinks, until he hears the sound. It is like gas passing through an entrail, ending in a suck. He is wide awake. What is a suck doing in his kitchen? He strides almost angrily into the pale, moonlit kitchen and sees motion in the sink's black orifice. *Sssfz-ssffzs-uck.apop*! Again. He smiles and looks back into the bedroom. How can she sleep? *Apop*! How he distinguishes that shapeless bubbling in the drain he knows not. But he sees an obscenely bubbling sore, purely writhing in digestive juices. His own entrails seem to sink, and the first wave of terror passes over him. He rushes back to bed, and in the morning, the vindictive white light finds him wound into the sheet like a corpse.

Months, years after, his feeding has varying forms, rhythms, textures. He is obsessed with different parts of her body as, so slowly, he devours them. The terrain has expanded all the while he consumes it and more than once, he has looked at the sky at night and seen sunlit pores on the black, infinite body of a woman.

Once, for a holiday, she served herself to him minced, and he worshipped her. Yet, another presence begins to stir in the colorless terrain. Whereas food, in hills and valleys, dark, moist crevices and tangles, is always there—its basis is starvation. He can—he will—devour her.

Often now, he holds her late at night and long delays his bite. He is impossibly hungry and impossibly tender. One long dark night, she will not be with him: he will have consumed her. As they lie together, they dream of another form of being: the thing that only grows, does not age or die—a child. The creature enters their minds through the half-light, restively seductive, as round and full as a pink porcelain jug. Malleable, delectable, food until the end of their lives. They inhale great breaths of it and begin to plan. Karen stops contraception and months later when he feeds, her breasts are milky.

Many years have passed. Eric and Karen are again making love in another bedroom, at least three times the size of the earlier room. Of Eric's profuse associations to Karen's delectably edible form, not one remains. He is impotent with her if not feeding. Yet his thoughts are even more extravagant: he can simultaneously plan his career for a decade, consider the quarterly report cards of his children, achieve sexual satisfaction, and take one bite after another out of his wife. At this point, he does not truly know he feeds; feeding is the curve and resistance of reality. Karen always knows that she feeds, but so peoples the scene that she no longer knows it is Eric who feeds. She is a woman, a mother, the giver of nourishment; feeding is the pressure and shapelessness of reality.

Karen's thoughts form a catalogue. While Eric roots, she lists all that she has gained to herself as well as what she lacks and when she will acquire it. Every object in their home parades gravely through her mind and as each passes away, she mentally cleans and polishes it. Now she sees the new carpets in the living room: they are symmetrical Navaho pastels, more subtle and expensive than the Chinese rugs she considered, less imposing than the Bangkok designs. The rugs will remain in her thoughts, immense sponges of wordless matter, unless placed in a scheme of greater and lesser value. She moves on to the kitchen utensils, which pass in a faster, more sparkling train, then comes to the mops and brooms of the basement, which move with an awkward, laborious tread, like reptiles.

When she can remember an eating utensil in enough detail to distinguish it from others, she is thrilled. She has held it back from the void; she has saved it, nourished, gained it. She is the mother; she holds her home and family away from the great devourer, the nameless, gluttonous thing that turns the earth into an obscenity. What this thing is she does not know, for her thoughts remain a catalogue, an ancient reflex that dispels the warping of her vision, and the devourer is not contained by a bright page. Rarely does she now see two homes, two husbands; the parade of her possessions melds them.

Now Eric has taken a wedge from her thigh and is chewing contentedly. Karen has come to the pots and pans: great cauldrons wind dully before her eyes, skillets, stir spoons, knives, implements to cut, grate, curl, and whirl. Eric is also lost in his thoughts, which are not unlike those of his wife. He ponders the web-like blackness of 3:00 A.M., a time when he is often awake. There is a monster living beside the drain in the kitchen—a bubbling black pit of digestion. The creature also shrieks from the hills beyond his home. It is a huge, sordid mouth, a bit of whose tongue crawls up through the drain. Of this he is convinced, yet he has never mentioned it to anyone. As he lies beside his wife, munching his last little morsel, the fear is beaten back, and his thoughts are nearly empty of it. He closes his eyes for a small moment of paradise.

Karen will shortly serve dinner, which is already prepared in the kitchen. She knows that Eric is increasingly disturbed by the sight of raw food, and the agoraphobia he has long suffered from is exacerbated by it. He has not entered the kitchen in months. She pleases him by elaborate food preparation, creating meals that do not seem to be food at all, but mounds of some fabulous synthetic substance. She has bought many appliances; she has prepared malted meats and shattered vegetables; she has added coloring to make her dishes red, orange, purple. She has also severed three fingers in her new appliances and served them to her family. Tonight, dinner is composed of numberless multi-colored hors d'oeuvres, arranged in obsessively repeating layers like a Tibetan temple. Eric's eyes become moist, boyish, and trusting in the presence of such food. Again, the burden of 3:00 A.M. leaves him.

Son and daughter are walking down the long corridor to join their parents for dinner. The hall is huge and imposing, like all the life given to them by the giants they call their parents. Their house is cavernously immense, a true giant's abode, because their father is a vice president at his firm, they know. They also know that giants are omnipotent and can gobble them up at will. Yet they do not, for children are physical extensions of giants, making their great mouths and hands reach through time as well as space. Rather, the giants play with them like sacred toys, and the children always lose, for all games are lost by the weak and the beautiful. Children, they know, are palely beautiful, slug-like, and weak. The most beautiful things on earth are the weakest, destroyed inevitably by giants. Fear and beauty are always with them, an aspect of air. Fear is their true parent, they believe. It is a quiet, earnest presence that walks down the hallway with them. They know the dead, gray eyes of Fear; the dull sound of its heels in the hallway; the dry hands. The hand of Fear slips into theirs day and night. It will always walk down the long, dark hallway with them, and what gives them comfort is terror made tender.

Long ago, they found another true parent. It was a child's day like any other, made purely of impulse—the matter that gusts, whirls, and returns like spokes on a great wheel that is life. They looked over a river bank and saw tumult reflecting: windy currents, tear-drops of green, a forest in shadow-eaves, sunlight in streams, layers. Plethora. Yet under and through a thing wavered, made of light and wind, a wondrous tangle of disorder: the face of the World.

The World had a broad, dark brow, eyes glitter-black with something of humor and ferocity both, hair that was cloud-like, and the jaws of a beast. When they ran, the World rolled beneath their feet like a ball, and when they rested, it was upon the World's tremulous cape of flesh. When they were hungry, they pressed their lips to the warm, black lips of the World—the great jug-like, furry jaws—and milk passed between their mouths. And when love filled them, they lay down and felt the black lips and the earth's breath passing over them.

Life is the body orienting in space; it is not time. The World presses close; is sentient, feels as a child does. Its eyes dart from trees, clouds, grasses; they are open day and night. The World speaks in a coarse, disjunct voice by day but at night, its voice is a velvet roar. It is as beautiful as a child, and it can be destroyed by giants. If they awaken at night with their blankets fallen low on their thighs, the World runs its rough, cat-like tongue over their bodies and loves them.

The World is as filled with terror and dark places as with love, and strangest of these are elfin realms where toys speak, mountains move, and huge beasts bay. These live, yet they are somehow inauthentic and do not truly exist. Their mother is the first step into the elfin realm; she has given birth to them yet she is inauthentic. Many things live in the elfin realm: people who do not look like them, houses smaller than theirs, mothers, toys, gods, animals, water, grass, forests. Because they do not exist, the things of the elfin realm can be destroyed by giants. Their mother is destroyed both by their father and by herself, they know. The elfin realm may arouse feeling, yet never true regard or comprehension because it can be freely destroyed. The keeper of the elfin realm is their father; only he knows what is inauthentic. The things of the elfin realm feel both grave and foolish, for nothing denied existence can be content or serious. They are the most beautiful things on earth.

As son and daughter pass the living room, they see their mother's paintings, which seem like shrieks in delirious color. One group of paintings shows tables cluttered with food in opulent curves and thick strokes.

The people sitting before them are timid, wraith-like, insubstantial. These paintings, her earliest, are understandable to them. They know that the people are children, though no one has told them this. Karen's later paintings, of which there are fewer, disturb them. One cluster has gross enlargements of the surfaces of food. The world's flesh is suddenly all pits, flecks, grooves, aberrations. The latest paintings, fewest of all, show skeletons which fade into desert storms and sandy hills. A knife of white light pierces the world, and beneath it all forms collapse and vanish into background elements. In these later paintings, their mother is a stranger, dangerous and remote.

They know that their mother has the loveliness and sorrow of a thing that does not exist, yet their love for her is as intense as their love for the World. She wants to paint yet does less and less, they know. Instead, she wanders throughout the house and garden, enumerating and cleaning. She removes all garden plants from the soil, places them in her mouth, then reburies them, leaving a large black stain over her lips. They have seen her place vegetables into her vagina, then replant them. All things must submit to the logic of doing and undoing, as she herself does; of this she bears witness, metes out creation and destruction, transforms and devours.

She is inexplicably gone from the house for long periods, often riding the subway pointlessly, and once they found her sitting happily with six mannequins in a store window. Her back to the window, she poured seven tiny demitasses of tea, an exacting hostess. They pounded on the window and called to her, but she was lost in a social triumph. She is a large child who once existed yet does no longer, and they give her the devotion due one of the world's most beautiful, tortured things. They have always known she would be devoured.

As the family sits down to dinner, the children know they must speak first. They begin to utter the restricted observances they have learned from their parents. They make few references to action and generally describe what they have received from others. If they do not, their father's agoraphobia and mother's mouthing of objects will be exacerbated. More and more statements begin with "I" until what they say is a collage of impressions joined by nothing but I. This lulls both parents mysteriously. It is a sign that their children will indeed be like them.

The children must never mention their mother or father as such—the giants are an agency reviewing their experience, distinguishing what is significant and insignificant for them. As they sit before the table, it seems to the children as though they are being converted into food in a chant-like beat; this process has the hypnotic rhythm of their happiest childhood experience.

Son and daughter are developing a decided awe of food. At the table, they manipulate it in various artful ways and even compete with one another. Now, son has made an intricate necklace of twenty tiny beads out of his mashed potatoes. Daughter has made a village of teepees out of her green beans. Father and mother are pleased to see this preoccupation and believe it reveals their children's maturing emotions.

Mother is a hole in the texture of dinner table conversation. She emits a stream of observations about her family, house, and garden, placing all in schemes of relative value with other houses, gardens, and families. It is a background current to her family, meaningless but necessary, the boundary against all that is significant becomes manifest. This lulls the children, who love chanting and litanies. Father tells mother that she is trivial, excessively concrete, feminine—which allows her to know she has fulfilled her purpose.

As they play with their food, son and daughter ponder the mysteries of the elfin worlds. The contradiction of their mother's maternity and non-existence casts much of what they learn in doubt. They know that there are unreal people and unreal substances, like water (why it changes shape and goes down a drain). There are real children living in the unreality of childhood (why they play with toys). True experience will only begin when they are adults, and they often detest the toy-like, diminutive beauty of children. The unreal things are terribly imbued with fear and beauty, for they can be destroyed instantaneously by giants. They dare not mention the World to any giant. Mother sees their confusion and the pathetic state of the elfin worlds. She pities her children. She knows she does not exist nor did she ever, truly, believe that she would.

The food has now been eaten or turned into non-food. Mother has droned, and father has accused her of triviality again. Both relax and feel content with their performance as parents. The family has now arrived at the true purpose of dinner. Father suddenly looks embarrassed, then crawls under the table. Mother and children follow, gravely. The dark below is hot, moist, like the deepest shiftings of thought, endless in possibility. Mother removes her light shift, and her family begins to gnaw on various parts of her body.

While they partake of the mute, dark ecstasy, mother begins to apologize. She reveals, again and again, her guilt that she should possess so much significance, while not existing. She catalogues the oddities and contradictions she has engendered. Father is appeased by his second wifely meal of the day. Son and daughter are deeply grateful, since they know their normal development depends on this contradiction in their mother. If she were not simultaneously nourishment and non-existence, they would become strange in untold ways, even monstrous. They believe that a human being can become a monster. The earth is secretly pervaded by sordidness, and their mother saves them from it.

Mother stares at her body, half of which has now been devoured. Then she looks hungrily from face to face, triumphant. No one returns her glance. They cannot watch her as she smiles so voluptuously, runs her hands over the missing flesh, her fingers at last pressing, hard and rhythmic, upon her genitals, which are perfectly intact.

Dinner is over, and each family member goes to his own room. They feel empty and absorbed at once, as though a wave has passed over them. Mother clears away the dishes and remains in the kitchen. This is the happiest moment of her day. Her marriage and family are granite, a monument. There is no monstrosity in her home, no warping of her vision to refute her happiness. She gives the drain an accusatory glance; it neither writhes nor guzzles. She hugely pities women who do not have families, whose husbands are not vice presidents, and returns to her catalogue: this is what she has, that is what she lacks. She plans for the fulfillment of all imperative lacks.

Father returns to his computer simulations. The mild screen is his fond, diminutive rectangle, a reduction that pleases him more and more. His agoraphobia is so intense that he rarely leaves home now. His infrequent appearances at work, coupled with constant electronic commentary to other terminals, enhances his prestige as a vice president. He removes everything from the screen. Now is the perfect moment of his day. He enters no data into the terminal and passively watches the greenish light, which waits for him with the absorption and delicacy of a lover. It waits purely, exactly, with such evenness of energy, a complete negation of self, a caress. And then the hot loveliness swells his genitals. Such simple, naked, electric intensity. That is what she is, he thinks. She.

His eyes never off the screen, seeing nothing but the voluptuous green haze, his fingers slowly circle his fly. She would have the lightest touch, like this, if she could touch him. A groan of pleasure reverberates. Still the softest touch, but faster now. The image in his mind is a catastrophe, volcanic, fire: *she* gives this to him. Everything that comes from her is the simplest, starkest image—the shape of her ardor. The earth heaves. His breath comes rougher and faster. Now he can even think of the beast outside, foaming in the volcano. Long delayed, he at last unzips the magnificent hot candle, a froth already running down the side. And he rests, his candle lying out, small and tender now, naked over his abdomen. She would want that, he thinks.

Daughter is lying in her bedroom, amidst a great, pulsing rhythm that leads to the future. Again and again in the chanting beat of childhood bliss, she knows the loveliness of starvation. The ecstasy of the beat, the repetition, can make the woman for whom it is true, and so it beats—drum after drum, the thought, the future, as one. So the child embraces the woman and now, with her belly full, engenders a woman who loves starvation, the woman of the future. For a child is monstrous in this way—repetition can transform it limitlessly—all the while the child beats, chants, and is happy. That the future is devoid of pleasure has no consequence; ritual is greater than time.

Months ago, her parents sent her to a man who they said would help her. The man had pieces of paper framed on the wall—a sign of the elfin realm—which aroused her suspicion. Then she saw the death in his eyes. This man would bridge the gulf between childhood and womanhood for her. She knew this as she saw his tired, dead eyes, dead since the beginning of the world. It is wisdom in his eyes, she thought. She could trust him, for he would be as strong and cruel as a bridge between these worlds.

He removed her clothes, slower as her breath came fast, and then demanded that she lie still before him. She was frightened, but she did what he wanted. To the death in his eyes, she spread her legs widely apart, and her fear melted into pleasure. They were both part of a huge process, one that rose from the world's beginning like a huge, dark tree.

She looked in his eyes and knew that he had seen the world die, oh how many times! He was the oldest creature on earth. He drew out a plate of food and offered it to her. When she reached, he pulled it away. He did this many times until she screamed, then he plunged his hand into her genitals—to the end of all girlish secrets and silences—and moved his hand deftly, expertly, as it had been done for eons. It gave her the greatest pleasure she had ever known. When he removed his hand, her childhood fled in its lovely red cloak. Now, she no longer needed him.

Mother is in the garden for a last count of her vegetables. She has removed each plant from the soil for one hour, placed it in her mouth, then replanted it for the night. The undoing of the given is so powerful to her that she no longer knows she engages in this nightly activity. Lately, there is a strange taste in her mouth. Sometimes, she places a flower in her mouth, and an obscenity comes back out. Obscenities are powerful growing things that can replace the flowers in her garden, she believes. Their blossoms are squat, round, and full of twitches —disturbingly soft and wet to the touch— forming unpredictable curved clusters that confuse and frighten her. She knows this as compellingly as she knows the eyes of her husband and children. Upon contact with an obscenity, you no longer know where boundaries are, she thinks. You might fall into it. Her breath comes in fast, terrified gasps. They are portals, eerily curved and soft, into another world, perhaps hell. If she accidentally places one in her mouth, digestive juices burst out and roll down her chin. She closes her eyes in agony. Nothing is safe if obscenities can bloom like this.

In the waning light, she tills and hoes the soil, pulls out the weeds and obscenities, and the obscenities grow back in abundance. When did they begin? When was the first? she asks. Her mind catalogues itself, but there are no causes and effects, beginnings or endings, in a catalogue. A handful of black obscenities springs wickedly up at the edge of her vision, their petals waving rhythmically, insidiously. How can the garden of a vice president be invaded so easily? she wonders.

It is enough if her family never notices the obscenities, she thinks. They have penetrated the house only once. The children picked a bouquet of flowers and placed it in the living room. And there, between two lustrous, innocent roses, she found the obscenity leaking a pool of liquid! She put it into her mouth, chewed, and swallowed. Only by absorbing it could she be certain of its destruction. In a whisper, she thinks: obscenities are tortuously subtle. You would think you were only looking at a garden, a house, a child . . .and there is motion! A pool of liquid, a panting of rhythm, the flower melting horribly in your hand . . .

Even thinking of it now, in the garden, in the dark air, and the green plants becoming gray, melting into invisibility, her breath comes fast. She must be more vigilant. Much more.

Years pass. It is 3:00 A.M., and son and daughter are sleeping, almost a young man and woman. It is the age of dreams, premonitions, visitations, hauntings—creatures of gauzy, shadowy substance, light and quick as desire. A dream torch illuminates their rooms, liquidates the walls; their beds become transparent and they hang in air, soundless dreaming birds, pendant above wonder and terror.

Father is curled into a huge, grainy ball on the floor beside the kitchen, listening to the nightly chorus of sucks, squawks, and escaping gases that rise from the drain. These sounds caress him with softly probing fingers of pain. At last he returns to the bedroom, touches the remains of his wife—a silent claw and a vagina—and he drops, rock-like and oblivious, into bed. The family is continually severed and reunited by the savagery of its dreaming desires.

A figure enters the rooms of son and daughter. With the fierce, white ray of thought, it pierces the walls of their dreams and enters, whole, into another logic. The figure moves slowly, rhythmically, languorous as dreams and compulsions.

It is an angel. They know this instantly, though they are asleep. The white light has appeared many times in their mother's paintings. As the light passes over them, their genitals stir and then swell.

The angel's face is palely exquisite, ice-cold. She offers her hand, but they do not take it. Tears continually roll down her white cheeks; they shudder and fall in designs of intricate crystalline beauty. I am the angel of thought, the figure tells them. Your lives will now end and begin again. Time has come into being and transformed space to a vast cosmic cube filled with hovering, dancing shadows.

And they see it: the faces, gardens, forests of their childhood flee. All form, motion, light is drawn into the cube and transformed. Mirroring the dark and dreaming earth, the cube has a luminous, blue ceiling dotted with star-like striations of light; below it, all of life has become soaring images, dancers rising and floating in air. Son and daughter remember the face of the World. Its eyes have long been closed: green profusions of vine curl over them, and its lips are gray and heavy, putrifying. The angel tells them that she will be all the World has been to them and more. Their lives will now be filled not with the world but its images, magnificent thought-images that rise into air like dancers, turning forms that soar, glide, and never again touch ground.

Son and daughter find themselves within the cube; the room in which they dream is now a painting that sleeps, dark and gravid, upon the wall. Ephemeral shapes fly past them, float—lighter than air, than light—each with the face of the angel. The angel watches them with the eyes of thought, pale and numberless. The earth, they see, is now the sum of these dancers who turn and glide in the dance of the universe. Never again will they look at the earth and see a face; never will the World be alive to them. Now their eyes will rise to the realm of thought's dancing eloquence: soaring images, a universe charged with their airy power. In such images is the only love and beauty they will ever know.

Great shudders carve the angel's face, and a gleaming line of blood breaks from her mouth. Their father, they see, is filled with this angel, and she confers power upon him. Son and daughter now understand that they will have this power. They, too, will be giants, with the freedom to destroy the elfin realm: all that is inauthentic to thought. And the earth dances, reels; turning and leaping in air is thought.

The dancers have become the World. On they sleep, in the deepest springs of the mind.

When son and daughter awaken, a new way of knowing lies coiled in their entrails. Each feeding, they see, must be majestic, bounded by a fortress without windows. Like their parents, they will be devourers, for when they can no longer consume, they become limp, raw food. That is the monster twitching behind the window shades, the sordid thing that bubbles in the kitchen. The world beyond the fortress is made of raw food, and the spirit that wanders in its wastes has a bottomless hunger that demands their devouring, their rendering into its own inanimate design. Design is ruler of the world, hungriest of all, devourer of all they can conceive.

Toward this monstrous nature, the family feels a radiant scorn—their truest, most fertile bond. Father and mother are proud to see derision illuminating their children's faces: it means they have become adults. Son and daughter feel the gravity of their calling to scorn, the social intercourse of giants, its varieties and contexts the subtlest of all feeling. It is far better, they see, to devour than to love the elfin realm.

It is now shortly before dinner, and son and daughter wait outside their father's study. The world has two poles—father's study and mother's dining room. Dwellers of the hallway, shadows, they are too poor to own doors that can be closed. The angel's promises have not yet been fulfilled, leaving a pit of rage in their entrails. Now, beyond their father's door, they hear the world's machine roar: rumbling wheels, crackling gears, a plane's streaking shriek across the sky. A terrible purposiveness, a will utterly diverging from their own. Their old friend, Fear, still walks behind them, its cool hand slowly enclosing theirs, a gentle, annihilating mystery. The shadows of childhood still sweep past them, impish gusts of wind. Will the angel ever destroy Fear? they wonder without hope.

Safety is force over their parents, and they note with fascination the skin of father and mother, utterly unlike their own: lumpy, sprawling, a livid sprinkling of acid caught in fleshy folds. This crumbling tissue reminds them of their mother's abandoned paintings. The children see the glimmerings of raw food springing from their parents, the end that will one day seize them and shake, leaving nothing but wastes of limp matter. Their own ends seem impossibly distant; they grow regardless of feeding, magically transformed. The length and richness of their days is one of thought's most brilliant images, the dancer who floats on the soundless trajectory of eternity. They will live forever, they think, and reach beneath their clothing to caress themselves.

Inside the study, father runs computer simulations throughout the day and much of the night. They see a greenish face lit by a screen, a blanched shape that makes the cycles of dark and light irrelevant. His agoraphobia has expanded to include all that lies beyond the fortress. He has not left it in years. Though his home is a windowless cavern, he delights in wearing a blindfold. The most intense life rests in his huge, blunt fingers.

His simulations now encompass issues of greater and greater breadth—the equations of starvation, catastrophe, cosmology, love. The world without is that obscenity, raw food, hence his simulations are the only reasonable approach to it, he thinks. Manipulation from a distance is the proper relation to a nature so monstrous: this is self-apparent, the algorithm of living itself, he believes.

As he completes a series of requests to the screen, his hand circles his fly. He is impotent if not sitting in this chair. His thoughts pass to the formulations and equations he has entered into the terminal and their rationale: She desires it. The heat of her passion is abstract equivalence. With it, he woos her, gorges, defecates. The ground breaks, rising to mountains, catastrophe. Faster and faster he circles his fly, groans loudly once in the force of his own fluid. Then he hears the snicker. The hallway often holds such tenuous, obscene laughter.

A rare moment of spontaneity: he removes his blindfold, opens the door, and stares at his children. They see the great gashes and folds of their father's face; an oozing chuck of meat, a primitive mask. Beneath his eyes are full, round pockets holding excrescences of power. The ancient clock is within him, they know; it moves him inexorably toward the end.

Father can scarcely recognize his children: so glowing, new, so penny-bright are they. He has nearly forgotten that flesh can be this. He pulls a pinch of his daughter's cheek out, lets it rebound like rubber. He owns this flesh; he can let it settle back into its habitual pig-eyed hostility. The girl's eyes travel down to the stain over his genitals and she thinks, the touch of this wet meat stick is my father.

A snarl of laughter nearly overpowers the whine of machinery. Father knows that his children aren't the source of such cold, derisive laughter: he has given them too much. He puts the blindfold back over his eyes and reaches for his invisible assailants. The children lead him down the hallway wondering, as well, where these vicious claps of laughter come from. They see their own faces twisted with hilarity, soundless and pure. All briefly unite in pride at the hallway's expanse: what a chance son and daughter have to scorn that murderous presence outside their fortress, how powerfully and materially father has resisted it.

The children are indeed proud as they lead him: he is now mayor of the city. But what is that, they wonder. A mayor is a spitting loudspeaker in the street. It is a man who raises his arms before a crowd on a blinking monitor or in the cruder black and white visceral layers of newspapers. The photos are facts, they know, but their meaning is part of the elfin world that animates the T.V. screen, drops pieces of meat into the newspaper, and is all that is left of mystery. The elfin realm controls all contact with the world of giants, hence the children's doubts are as universal as their father's agoraphobia. To his supremacy, they toy with sand-castles of nihilism beyond anything he can conceive and laugh in quietly murderous childish hearts. It is fitting, they think, that this man whose skin sprouts lumps and crevices as the years are lost should be the mayor of raw food. This thought ends in mid-air, a dancer. Do they detest their father? Does a dead king reign over a dead kingdom? No, they are lost in an image without cause or effect, the mind's exquisitely floating matter.

The children and their father enter the dining room: another time and place, mother's domain. They hear no whining machinery here—it is almost perfectly silent. The walls and furniture are covered with tiny, convoluted lines. It is a wild, fairy script, the handwriting of a child. The totality is their mother's enumeration of every object she has gained and ritual completed, all that has been saved from the devourer. It is also a language, and they know that this child, their mother, is trying to communicate. She says something about food, life, death, and the devourer, but no one can decipher this alien tongue. Who would know more, they think, about the world of raw food than their mother? Yet they scorn the monstrosity she daily translates, the immense pressure beyond the fortress that wants nothing better than to turn them into raw food. How can they listen to a starving wraith, howling at them from the wastes of raw food? Mother knows this: they will never understand her language or the beast beyond the fortress. Rather, they will scorn her, which makes her intensely proud: it means her children are adults. Her family is strong.

The room is full of obdurately bright light. The children shade their eyes and see, at last, their mother. A throne covered with script is in the corner; a twitching patch of dry skin sits upon it. They can barely make out her legs—lying askew, an obscenity—a pair of hips, an arm that reaches out like a claw, weaving back and forth, continually in motion. To the claw, they owe this incomprehensible script.

The children and their father feel like giants and wonder whether the diminutive room holds enough air for them. No one, they know, can live comfortably in this space but their mother: she does not exist, and this consummate lack has a life and dimension of its own. They are awed by the energy in mother's fingers as they slither over the throne; her arm is a crustacean scuttling up and down the wall, tirelessly covering it with diminutive script. Yet she prepares their food, feeding them with her own body, they know. She is the eternally pregnant myth passing between worlds—life and death, raw and cooked—and they owe their lives to her.

Sumptuous is the banquet before them! Mounds of intense coloration heave themselves, apocalyptic as mother's abandoned art: torrid layers with rounded domes, lascivious tongues, carnivorous blossoms that seem to lap the air, fabulous nests with branches roiling in all directions, undulating waves of pink, green, white, black. It is impossible to distinguish food of any kind: the obscenity has been destroyed. This banquet might be alive; if not, it could be boiling liquid, soap, yarn.

The family sits before the dinner table, paying homage to mother. Yet all watch father, who must lead them. Father grabs a great, doughy, pinkish mass and fiercely pounds it to a puddle. Son and daughter follow, pluck mounds of colored fluff and smash them to puddling rainbows. In ecstasy, mother's claw moves faster and faster. Destruction intoxicates, and all want to cry out in joy.

Yet mother's world has its own power; it resists them. The bizarre walls sink inward, their limbs are clutched by script, their arms and legs smash huge holes in the walls and from these crevices, monstrous beasts push their gnarled heads and lantern jaws into the room and bay! Now: Great, blackened snouts, cascades of hoary fur, huge fiery horns and feral hooves cry out again and again as more fluff is flattened. Ecstasy has seized the family like a predator. They smash the food again and again, the florid puddles stream over the table, and larger holes are wreaked in the walls. The world is an ecstasy of destruction while the monsters roar and roar.

Mother is proud to see her banquet destroyed. She knows that all she accomplishes will be destroyed, even her own essence, and by what better hand than that of her family? The food is now pulp, barely distinguishable as solid or liquid. Mother's claw is still. They feel calm, nurturance, stasis.

The great beasts are silent, the air hot with fetid breath. The family stares at this room of immensely black, monstrous faces—wild, reddened eyes and tangled coils of hair; vast, gaping mouths with pike-like teeth and furry lips. The family's hearts are full and satisfied; they are grateful to these beasts who have trumpeted the joy of destruction. Slowly, the monstrous faces recede into a bloom of fiery light, sink back to hell, their velvet hooves at last vanishing into brimstone soup.

Son and daughter reach into their clothing and inspect their bodies for signs of monstrosity. They see smoothly spare, androgynous parts. No, only their mother is a monster. They caress their soft nakedness. Perhaps, the family thinks, they all do love one another. Perhaps they always have. They are father, mother, son and daughter. Who can deny their love? Only the voice from beyond these walls—and how empty and hungry this voice must be, how false and unreal.

The true purpose of the meal obtrudes itself. Father asks them all to disrobe, then leads them under the table.

The dark, below, is filled with new tastes, scents, colors, a broth of liquid pungency in swells of undulant red and purple. The warm liquid flows over the children, leaving lovely electric pins on their arms, legs, torsos. It enters their mouths and swirls about their genitals, which redden and swell to huge proportions while thrusting rhythmically.

Father looks at these newly firmed genitals contracting upon such lithe, otherwise androgynous bodies and breaks into a clap of jeering laughter. His own body, massive and sinewy, towers over them; his genitals, though soft, are immense. Though they are young and he is old, all understand that he is superior, with every right to dominate their lives. Youth counts for nothing beside this fatherly beast. The faces of son and daughter are transfixed by passionate hatred. They know the purpose of feeding has changed with the years. Their father now initiates them into young manhood and womanhood. For this, they despise him.

The children watch their uncontrollable genitals in horror—purplish, of terrifying proportions, thrusting—while the beast that is their father laughs again and again. Whatever this process is, the children cannot stop it. It is within them.

Father and mother proudly inspect the genitals of son and daughter while the children cower on the floor. The pelvic thrusts create a rhythm the children have always known: the chanting beat of childhood bliss, of oblivion. Is this what bodies must do, they wonder? Is this what childhood has prepared them for, genitals that gorge and starve uncontrollably? The thought is one of the swiftest dancers, an image that floats, never to touch ground again. They have no sense of its origin and will never believe it.

Father grabs a piece of mother's thigh and watches them darkly as he gnaws, foams, and swallows. The obscene laughter surrounds him, and his children cannot look at him. The beast is unconcerned, rests comfortably on his hairy elbow, is nurtured and appeased, then tears off a piece of flesh for his son. Now both father and son are eating, visibly relaxed. Father offers a piece to daughter, who reaches for it and is shoved aside. This happens several times, and both father and son break into raucous laughter. Daughter lies on her side watching them eat, the strip of moist flesh between her legs swelling even larger. Her hunger is a thousand delicious little knives striking her body at once, then forming a fist of pressure over her genitals. She longs to be touched and abused by these rough male hands. Her legs part reflexively, begging for rape or starvation. This comforts her: to resist is to be monstrous.

Father is darker and hairier now, a beast feeding upon another beast. The children understand that this is the greatest pleasure they will ever know. They caress their slim, unresisting bodies again to see if horns and fur have sprouted like horrible tubers. No, they are not monsters. Only their mother is always a monster. They caress themselves again and again, their hands passing lingeringly over their hugely swollen genitals. As mother watches them, a calm comes over her. She, too, is relieved that only she will be the monster. Her claw passes over the remnants of her body and comes to rest inside her vagina, still perfectly intact. Like those of her children, mother's genitals are swollen and reddish. Her eyes close in deep harmonic appreciation: so human life passes from one generation to another, she thinks.

In a moment, each family member lies in a separate room of the house. Do father and son know they have fed upon mother? Do mother and daughter know it? No, the dancer that is their sustenance has already glided past them, soared to the realm of images, breaking the earthly bond of cause and effect. The family no longer knows the origin of its thoughts and will never believe what it has done. Now mother can be devoured whole; now she may vanish, which she deeply desires.

Father returns to his computer simulations. Son and daughter lie in their bedrooms, their thoughts filled with images that make their genitals swell again and again: gorging and rape, starvation and ecstasy. These thoughts are some of the most beautiful they have ever encountered: lightest and swiftest of dancers, images floating in the mind's airy torrent without gravity or cause. Where have these images come from? they wonder. How have they grown into young adults with such mysteriously active genitals? They will never know. They are the young man and woman their parents desired, hypnotized by the mind's floating images, beautiful and untrue.

Mother is out rolling in the vegetables. Her garden, full of plant-like, pulsating shapes, is now nothing but obscenities, providing her with limitless opportunities for scorn. She extirpates the obscenities violently with her claw, parts their meandering roots, then drops them, twitching, into the dirt while peals of derisive laughter convulse her. It is her happiest moment of the day. By the end of the evening, the whole garden is a writhing liquid mass. Mother does not remember her former fear of obscenities. She knows they are her closest companions. As her eyes rise to the empty horizon, the earth of which she is a part seems radiated by swarms of delicate, twitching roots. A million baby hands seem to be reaching, clutching ... This thought makes her laugh uncontrollably, for what a chance has she, at last, to scorn this swarming plain, this world that has devoured her. Perhaps her own laugh is last and hardest, she thinks, for didn't she stuff that hungry earth with obscenities? Her children's mouths and hands are everywhere, lunging.

She rests, matriarchal gardener, in the midst of quivering, tuberous roots, heaves of liquid life, lapping shapes now vegetal, now animal: and sees how endlessly powerful is her family. How could it be else? On this bedrock of obscene fertility, tended by the utter obscenity she herself is, she knows that her family is superior to all others.

The dry little patch of flesh rolls all over her garden, heaves of derisive laughter shaking her claw. Yes, the day has been magnificent, she decides. She thinks of her children, almost adults, and how they caressed their own nakedness, how completely they rejected her. She is swollen with pride that she has such children and a husband who is mayor. How pathetic, she thinks, that all women are not like her.

The patch of flesh returns to the cavern. Its scurrying claw pauses in the living room to admire the empty canvases covering the wall. This is the final phase of her art, she believes; the blank surfaces are a deep, soundless chord to which her most intimate self, her nonexistence, resonates. They are the perfect embodiment of the vindictive white light that has long pursued her, the angel's light, the wondrous ray that can destroy anything. Her life has flowed inexorably to this ray, the thing to which she is utterly inimical, the blank, invisible sword that must fall on her. She is, after all, a creature who has never existed; therefore, she must disappear. And in the white light's blinding roar, the light that doubts all, that sees, for mother, a skeleton on a random background, she is finally vaporized. The light is an immersion, a thousand tiny knives full of pleasure, starvation of the whole being at once, and mother— only a vagina, not even a claw—vanishes into it, leaving her family in the purest, whitest light of perfection, superior to all families, bottomless in their scorn. Her last thought is: what finer gift could I have given them?

Many years pass. Father is now governor; mother was devoured years before. Father lies on his bed in a room immense, ornate, and ponderous. He is a sinewy wedge, rounding plummishly over the belly and coils of chin. A mane of white hair brightens his riven face like some strange, irrelevant dawn. Beside father lies a tiny, brittle, aged doll, mother's replacement. The creases and folds of its ancient face web suddenly around the mouth; a gleaming terror widens its eyes. As an effigy of a woman who never existed, it is a supreme artifice created by its own progeny. The doll's thought is slow, creeping, and shadowy as an old cat; it registers nothing but that its family is superior to all others.

Man and wife live in a tunnel miles within the earth. On the surface is their former home, now enclosed in rose-tinted glass, an artifact of feeding. Moving video cameras beside it scan all directions. These images and many other panoramas flood over ancient telephone wires on request and flicker constantly on father's monitors.

The architecture of this subterranean hole is simple. Each room has a video monitor covering two walls; a third wall is an orifice. All necessities of life can be drawn down to them by electronic requests, and the orifices are never empty. Father loves to place the doll tenderly on his knee and show it each new addition rumbling from an orifice; he knows this delights the doll.

Fiercely old is this father, crustily venerable, the most grizzled and paternal of elder statesmen. As governor, he has beome a visionary of landscape architecture, designed a plethora of projects in which the world is cast into a million dancing dots on his monitor. His agoraphobia and horror of raw food passed years ago to the very structure of his thought: his is therefore the supreme achievement of transforming the earth into his yearning, hungry image of it. Now, in his old age, the world has brilliant, new, non-functional shapes on the grandest scale: burgundy bridges rise miles above urban tracts; skeletal homes are erected from identical metal sheets; water now flows in numberless trenches over the earth, forming infinite designs of random erosion, trembling stripes of a racing zebra. There are deserts where sand has been compressed into blocks. There are urban festivities where cities are destroyed cathartically, metal balls that swing once and roar, demolishing walls. The audience has its most ecstatic sense of ritual and time from these carousels of destruction. Father creates charged atmospheres, he believes, towering forces like the great sculptures of Easter Island. He is very happy, and he knows the doll feels exactly as he does.

The family is intensely proud of him. In these flashing new forms of the earth, they drink the oldest mystery: the elfin realm of their childhood, the earth that flickers, shadows, is never known. The realm whose destruction is a hungry giant's right. Their scorn is now boundless, their one infinitude. How could father have failed to subjugate it? She, the woman in the monitor, demanded it, baubles for her love. She asked only images; they are her food, her love.

Of course, father reflects, there has been huge displacement and loss of life, human no less than plant life and wildlife. Yet this very earth finds his ideas impossibly seductive. She and father are wedded in their vision, brazen in its erupting newness: vast striped plains; an empty desert of blocks, wind shrieking for its lost medium; bridges that end only in the sky's cloudy mouth. How exquisite are these images, dancers born in mid-air, never touching earth, for the earth rolls, groans. It is too old for us. We do not want it.

There are no more simulations, he thinks. Now, there are imaginary facts.

Beneath it all is raw food, he knows: starvation, death, that murderous thing that will even devour him. Yet the world is now dappled, brindled, becoming glimmer; it no more reminds him of raw food than his wife's ancient, torrid meals.

His hole is so immense that he can't remember it, an ideal embodiment of intimate life, he thinks. It has acoustic and visual properties that disturb him, though. As he sits with the doll, to whom he is devoted, he can hear soft, strange echoes. The light is kept bright and punishing. He fears echoes and shadowy places—such web-like, haunted things! He doesn't want to be alone with these thoughts, and even sitting here with his wife, the doll, he is nearly alone.

He raises the image of his success to that obdurate light. Surely he is the greatest of devourers, his success massively materialized, his hole exorbitant. In the tunnel are rooms bathed in gold, in silver. His monitors can generate sixty million different shades of color. The doll is always beside him, and he has purpled her to ferocity, green'd her to innocence, dazzled her in celestial blue, and made her live in the hush of pure white arctic light.

He adores these ministrations, these excesses of love, and he is sure the doll adores them, too.

He reflects upon his beginnings: the slender, nervous young man who so long delayed that first morsel of his wife, who wondered whether he would ever hunger for greatness. And now, he is an old visionary of hunger, hunger for the whole earth—the equal, at times, of that murderous presence. Surely his life is a greater and greater synthesis, he thinks: the pin-striped earth, his tunnels and fortresses, the abandoned art of his child-like wife, this infinitely malleable doll which is her final shape. These divergences have coalesced: he is scientist and artist, husband and child, cooked and raw.

The doll is always silent in her terror. He prefers coloring her in rose or pure white. His thoughts of her perturb him. Sometimes, just at the edge of his vision, he sees her move. There is an edge to his power, somehow, and there she has her own mysterious life. She is only a doll, and this is impossible, he knows, but the thought goes wandering.

Once, he swore he saw her creeping on her stiff little doll's legs—painfully, hideously—there at the edge where she lived. She creeped like an injured thing before an uncovered wall, like the blank canvas that had once awed her. It troubled him to see—to think he saw—those tiny, distorted doll's fingers reaching up to the emptiness. He knows this perception is irrational, even mad—a doll can't live and move—yet those white daggers, her hideous little fingers still go reaching up, up into the blank air. What can she want so terribly? Is she not content with what he has given her? Can her empty, empty head contradict its own nature and dream of what she might have put on the canvas? Creepingly, horribly reach those little daggers!

But then, it is no more than tragedy, he decides, and the summing up of a life is that inevitably. Pity can never be justified. His bridges and deserts are summings up and though the earth may weep, he will not. These summings up are those evanescent dancers in mid-air, caught in their instant of light and halted, the limbs free and lithe as a lover's, hauntings of our lives, ghosts of the spirit. Here, in this rarified air, hadn't his wife led a beautiful life, always imbued with meaning?

There are moments, too, when he could swear he sees the faintest flicker of an expression on the doll's face! One of absolute intensity without object or end, frozen, as though a wave of poison touched all her veins at once. In this, he is sure she says she needs him—madly, impossibly. Another flicker passes over the doll's face, and he sees glacial perfection, arrogance, yet with such a delicate, child-like mouth! He is enchanted, and his hands move reflexively to part her legs.

Nothing but cool plastic lies beneath his thumbs. It has been years since he thought of that full, accepting body whose curved radiance he entered, gnawed. The comparison jangles with the doll's empty terror. He wants to be respectful, he reminds himself. This is the gift of his later life with her: he will be more humble, more tender.

One day, his gift exploded. He was looking through the video cameras around his former house. A jungle of vines and leaves was suddenly before him, the spot where his wife had lain with her vegetables. There in the soil, twitching, beside the roses, *twitching*! was a pale and horrid thing. A bit of tentacle, tiny and frail, twitched with hideous life. Its dry, starved, impossibly aged surface filled the camera. It was one of the most subtle, complex surfaces he had ever seen, a perverse little world turning before him. He felt assaulted, violated.

It reminded him of his wife, and worse. Was it not that eerie presence, the soul of raw food calling out, starving beyond his fortress in the wastes of the world? Was this shriveled patch not the monster who burbled in the bowels of the kitchen, a nightmare not of children but adults? His fingers clutched, the terminal went blank, and he watched an empty screen, wondering whether he had gone mad ...

Today, however, this horror is far from his thoughts. It is a holiday, and the family is reunited. The rich umber of late afternoon pours on his video cameras, nearly touches him with its heat. The mother doll is bathed in his favorite rose light. Majestically sits the family in its colossal hole, awaiting dinner, as ever. Son is a burly, massive man, prone to overweight and lust, yet masculine and rosy. The whole rippling surface of this giant is vibrant, down to the tiny trumpet of thick, curly hair disappearing beneath his cuffs. This is a fellow who grabs, bends, wolfs. He has sampled the shanks, breasts, hearts, thighs of many. When that deep voice rumbles from his massive throat, hardly a woman can resist feeding him with her body. A fine, appropriate son, his father thinks.

Daughter is more ambiguous. Something glacial and remote trembles in her eyes, perhaps the doll coming early. Yet what a magnificent, round bosom, shoulder, hip: what hunger she is made for! This daugher will last far longer than her mother, the final vindication of the plastic doll. There is some obsessive gnawing that father discerns about daughter's thighs. That perversely sensitive husband is to blame, he thinks, the little man who must take her in tiny, fierce bites. The children are more hale than their parents, a natural consequence of his power and success; he knows the doll shares this thought.

Food lies in identical metal containers; the meal is now perfunctory. Their true nourishment shifts in the shadows beyond the fortress. While they pelt the walls with food, they remember the painful, perverse luxuriance, the gorging that was childhood. The light and breath of a family is the umber, stifling air of love. Son and daughter examine their bodies reflexively to see whether the monsters have become them but no, the beasts still lie prone, drooling and burbling in hell. When will the great horns, fangs, snouts, the hungry madness come to feed with them again? They do not know. Food, endless food is here—in their limbs, loins, breasts. It cannot be doubted, not yet.

A hefty man and woman thus sit before their brilliant father and stiffly ancient mother, remembering the gorging fulfillment of the home that once was, brimming with caverns and compulsions. Home and rest will always exist in these terms for them. Father rests his eyes on the future and wonderfully, it is the past. He feels the swell, the great rhythm and ritual of human life.

All stare in wonder at the doll, and their ancient awe creeps out, a tentacle of memory. It is, after all, she who has nurtured and sustained them. She is the myth vaporized between worlds: she has fed them with her own self, fallen and become a monster, risen and soared beyond life. Father flicks lights of many colors over her consummate, shriveled face—the last, the only one they could not devour. Of many hues now are her eyes, cool and wide as terror. She is violated in blue, in mauve, in amber. Daughter watches and fiercely longs to be raped and devoured. The doll's face is an ecstatic religious mask, an icon. Her genitals are perpetually swollen. Her life has been a passion, they believe.

They long, at last, for their own story to end, but it can only end with father. He is the sole character who truly, unequivocally, exists. Mother the ecstatic has never existed. Her children exist as phantoms, the fate of doubters and blasphemers. For them, there will always be monsters poised at the edges of things. Their flesh-food hides them now, but one day the gaping mouths will rise and gulp them whole.

Father, the one exigency, hides a secret and a vision. The secret, which his children can only guess, is that he is starving. He has been doing so since mother vanished and the doll came to give him her emptiness. His face is a barren planet of caverns, crevices, pits. Raw food now bulges fulsomely from his features, slumping down like tears. He is a human waterfall of flesh, of sorrow. The dark clock has gone beyond its hour.

What can feed him now? Once, he thought his children would. Or his success. Or *she*, the woman behind the monitor. That was the ultimate betrayal, for he fed her all his images. Now she flickers, dances over the earth in his fortresses and behemoths, yet the shade of starvation wanders at will. He is lost. Everything on earth leaves him hungry. He hardly even fears that restless, murderous presence. It is inside him, and its hunger is his own. He feels the munificence of his love for the doll, that he should love her even though she cannot feed him. Even love, he thinks, has been one of his great gestures.

His days are perambulations of the hunger within him. He watches the video monitors and imagines gorging on all he surveys. As drool oozes from his lips, the world becomes a greater and greater obscenity. The doll lies naked all the time, and one of her barely discernible, flickering expressions is whorish.

The hole is less and less comfortable for him now, though he complains but little since no one is there to listen. The air is full of spotlights, judgments, echoes. His face is always awash in the greenish glow of his monitors.

Of the many images that course over the wires is the comforting interior of a church. The building is magnificently preserved; ancient, dark walnut glows from it like a blessing. It is a pure artifact, like his fortress above. The audience is a mixture of the elderly, represented by video monitors, and young families, present in the gorging flesh. They are singing from hymnals now, and father has the strangest sense that he is falling in love—with image, sound, and light. He adores watching the old, grave faces on the monitors, the young, ringing bodies in the pews.

He returns to the church again and again. At first, it seems restful, but then he perceives a deeper significance. As his hungry eyes pass over it, the scene entices memory. The soaring vaults and arches are like the ribbed texture of his mouth's roof, and the spiritual effluvium is his own billowing saliva. He laughs when he discovers this relation. It is one of those disarmingly simple things one has looked for all one's life without knowing it: the summing up, the dancer rising on the wave of pure meaning. As he follows the upwardly sweeping arches of the church, his tongue now rises munificently to the roof of his mouth, pushes, then falls to the sacred altar, where the juices of his saliva rise and billow like the creation. What a religion of feeding this is, he thinks; communion is merely Christ's acknowledgment.

After the service, the camera moves to other rooms of the church and again, he finds that delectable grace he is seeking. A reception is held for the congregation and on plates passing throughout the crowd are numberless wives served minced. This scene fairly tingles with memory for father. He remembers when he and his wife were young, and she could not even wait for him to feed. She served herself to him, like these women. Yes, he feels more familiarity, camaraderie here than any place besides his hole. In every direction are hale, hearty, well-fed men and tender, erotic, gnawed women, their eyes a deliciously receptive blank. This room is the receptacle of his deepest wants.

He knows that these beliefs, these people, will feed him. Not real food, of course, but imaginary food, surely. Any entrance of the imagined is the entrance, as well, of his strongest, tenderest, most grotesque impulses. How fitting it is to see the end of his life here, the doll beside him.

He takes the doll into his arms and has the sense that at last, he truly sees her: that shock always ebbing in her eyes, the thing he'd thought was terror, mask, ice. He now understands it to be spiritual force. This little doll, its arms and legs splayed, violated, reaching out so chaotically, is very like Christ, he thinks. What greater image do we have of that wounded, murdered, eaten thing, our monster of the spirit?

His eyes pass again to the altar. He is the only character who exists unambiguously: he must therefore create meaning for others and now he does so, enraptured. The doll is also like that other sculpture on the altar, the virgin mother of God. Ice, pathos, rape shines from their eyes. So these three—mother, son, and doll—lived and were devoured in tenderest accord. The spiritual effluvia begin with their consumption; the end is the death of the earth, his own end. This thought is the last, most lovely stripe he wishes to paint on the world, now, when his old flesh droops. This is the meaning that rises, breaks into air, the exquisite, soaring thing, the purest thought, ghost to his flesh.